KINDLING

A COLLECTION OF SHORT STORIES

PAULA HARMON

Copyright

Dedication

This book is dedicated to my mother Christine and mother-in-law Patricia, who were the first to read these stories and are still speaking to me, even though they both feature in the stories.

***

Once there was a little girl who spent a lot of time alone. She sat under trees and sheltered in caves and hollows. She sat under bridges and looked downstream. She looked into mirrors and into books and out of windows onto storms crashing over the mountains.

She imagined.

She grew up.

But the child who looked for dragons is still inside the woman who looks out of the office window for something more interesting to think about.

She has never stopped imagining.

Contents

MIRROR GIRLS

One day, on her fifteenth birthday, my daughter will sit down on the floor in front of her wardrobe mirror and do her hair.

She'll do this rather than sit at the dressing table, because there will be make-up and chargers and all sorts over the surface and she'll say the light is bad and she can't see what she's doing, like she always does.

And she'll sit on the floor and do her hair and slowly brush it and try different styles and straighten it or curl it or whatever the in thing will be and she'll facetime her friend and ask her opinion and maybe she'll take a selfie and then she'll sit back, slumpy shouldered and look at herself properly. And she'll look at the light brown hair and wish it was darker or blonder and she'll look at the eyebrows she inherited from me and wonder whether to get them waxed or whether to try threading and she'll look at the nose and mouth she got from her dad and stare at her teeth wishing she'd got her dad's teeth instead of her mum's and she'll turn her head from side to side and wonder if she should get another ear piercing or maybe a nose piercing or whether mum will let her have her belly button pierced now, and she'll look hard at herself and wonder if she's ever going to look old enough to do stuff, remembering that both parents said they were twenty-two before they even looked eighteen.

And after a while she'll stop looking at her face and before long she starts contemplating her body. She'll look in the mirror itself and see what is reflected behind her - not what should be reflected: the dressing table and the bedside table and the teddy on the floor, but another mirror in a different wardrobe. Instead of seeing her own face, she'll see the back of a girl who is staring into another mirror just ahead of her and she'll see, in that other mirror, the reflection of the other girl's face. And she'll look a bit harder and she'll think 'I recognise that face. It's mine. No it's not mine, it's mum's only younger, like when she was my age'.

And she'll stare at the girl in the mirror who is me at fifteen. And she'll see me, staring at my own reflection and curling my hair and doing my make-up and considering the eyes I got from my dad and the nose I got from my mum and the mousy hair I got from who knows who (because I wanted to be a red head and it wasn't as if there weren't enough red headed genes floating about or maybe really dark like my mother). So my daughter will be looking at me when I was her age and watch me pause and stare into the mirror itself. Then my daughter will realise I am looking beyond myself into another mirror where, a young girl in a Guide uniform is plaiting really dark hair and trying on lipstick surreptitiously. And at the point that my fifteen year old self recognises the other girl, my daughter will realise that it is *my* mother, her grandmother and beyond *her* is another girl with auburn ringlets, barely visible, my grandmother, her great-grandmother and beyond that and beyond that...

And then, as my daughter stares into the mirror, back into the ancestry of girls staring at themselves, she will sense a movement and the dot in the distance will shift and then the next and then the next until she realises they are turning, one by one, to see what is behind them until she sees her great-grandmother turning to look at her grandmother, then her grandmother turning to look at me, then me turning to look at her. And hesitating, she will turn and see...

IN THE GARDEN

Seeing that article on slow news day brought it all back: things I'd forgotten; people I'd lost touch with; a village I'd left behind.

Dawn got on our nerves a bit. You know the sort: she said her dad had a really important job, although she wasn't sure what it was. They were always going to go somewhere really flash on holiday, but they never actually did. She said her parents thought books were more important than fashionable clothes. She could answer all those pointless questions teachers ask, but never knew anything about pop groups. As I say, she got on our nerves.

Of course, she also lived in the only house, apart from the manse, which was different to everyone else's. We all lived in semis. Ours were quite old, 1930s I think Mum said, but Dawn's house was older. It was detached and looked a bit lost. It stood on a sort of corner where the road coming up the hill split into two, like a Y. Her house was right there, right at the highest bit of the hill, looking down the hill and pretty much down on all of us. It wasn't a very old house. It wasn't spooky or anything. She said she thought it was Victorian, but Mum said it wasn't that old, it was just older than the rest and that a whole load of houses had been knocked down a long time before they built the estate. Mum said it was a good thing too: look at the few really old cottages that were left - barely room to swing a cat and so dark and damp. Some of them even still had outside loos and no bathrooms.

No, her house wasn't spooky. Dawn was a pain, but there only three girls the same age in our village and it got a bit boring hanging out at the slides and she did have a nice garden with a treehouse and her mum made good cakes, and didn't care how much mess you made and so we went round even though she never had any good records or anything. Sometimes she tried to tell us ghost stories but we wouldn't listen.

'Mum says that's all rubbish,' I told her.

'I know but...' she said, 'there's this woman....'

Sue said 'you haven't got a ghost, this house isn't old enough. Only really old houses have ghosts.'

'But honest, I see her in the garden. Sometimes she looks up at me. I swear, cross my heart.'

Sue and I sniggered. But we didn't go there after dark.

Well, we all grew up a bit and went to the comp. Dawn didn't show off as much anymore. There were lots of kids with posher homes and more money than hers and I think she realised what she'd sounded like and stopped. But she still sometimes went on about that ghost if people would listen. It was a shame she made it all sound so boring. If there'd been blood stains or screams, the other kids would have listened more, but no, just some drippy woman crying for no reason (which was sort of what you could imagine Dawn would do).

In Spring term the history teacher got us to start a project on local history as if normal history wasn't boring enough. Well to sum it up, glaciers made our valley U shaped (apparently), stone age people mostly made arrows, then Romans quarried for something, then later someone smelted something, then all that went away and left a boring village with nothing happening in which we had to live in.

Part of our project meant we had to interview the old people. The three of us went together to share the fun. Those old cottages smelt of damp and sometimes sickly, like something going bad. Mum said some of those old miners had a disease and it made them smell. They couldn't help it but we still felt queasy. The old ladies gave us dry old cake and told us about the war and the depression and poaching for rabbits and hoping the means testers didn't come round and what it was like working down the mines back when pay was really bad. The old men just sat and coughed. I think they were as bored as we were.

Actually Dawn wasn't. She wrote everything down and sometimes you could tell she was upset or angry about what they were saying. Sue just slouched back and rolled her eyes and I looked at the damp in the corners of rooms where these house-proud old ladies couldn't quite reach and nibbled at the dry old cake, longing to get out. Still, we could copy Dawn's notes later.

When we visited old Mrs Jones, it was with some trepidation. Since her husband died, people said, she had gone a bit doolally and couldn't be relied on to always know what year it was, let alone who you were, even though she'd known us all since we were born.

'You're from the big house, isn't it?' she said to Dawn.

'N-no,' Dawn answered, 'it's not that big, it's the same size as everyone else's,' she paused to look round the tiny cottage, 'well the same size as theirs,' she indicated me and Sue, 'it's just detached.'

Mrs Jones huffed and leaned forward, peering into Dawn's face. 'Manon: what you doing looking out of this girl?'

Sue sat up and Dawn leaned back. 'I'm Dawn, Mrs Jones, Dawn Roberts remember? From Forest Ridge. I'm Ceri's daughter. Remember? Ceri Davies she was.'

'Oh hullo Dawn,' said Mrs Jones, as if surprised to see us all sitting in her home, 'how's your mam? Why are you talking about the house on Forest Ridge?'

'We weren't,' retorted Sue, eyeing the door, 'you were.'

'Do you remember it?' I asked, 'the big house?'

The old lady appeared lost in thought for a while and then said, 'knocked down in the first war it was. I was about eight years old. It was a lovely house, ivy up the walls and lions on the gates. It was nicer than the manse even. Can you imagine? Nicer than the manse. Lemme see, I think I got a photo somewhere from before. This man came and did photos of all the villages and he got the local children to stand around to make it look interesting. We had to stand still mind. Only my brother Rob couldn't. He's a bit of a blur.'

She went and rummaged in a cupboard and brought out a beige picture of a biggish house with a small group of children standing in the road outside the gates. One of the boys was slightly out of focus.

She pointed at a small girl in a frilly white pinafore, her black stockinged legs planted firmly, her hand on a hoop. 'That's me.' she told us. 'It was a sad house. No-one was sorry when it was knocked down. Even Manon.' She said the name as if she hadn't uttered it before.

'Who was Manon?' asked Sue.

'She was the girl from the big house. Well not a girl really, she must have been thirty by then. But everyone thought of her as a girl. Her parents never let her do anything. Not after what happened.' The old lady stopped again, smoothing the picture as if she could will the people in it back to life and restore her own sturdy young body. 'See that's her father in the window there, you can just make him out. He was a one, he was. He didn't like common children like us outside the house. Wouldn't buy the photograph, he wouldn't. But my mam and dad did. It cost a bit, but see, it's not often they got the chance to get a photograph in those days and they were glad after because Rob went to the war and never came back and this was him to a tee, always on the go like. The picture the army took of him in uniform wasn't Rob at all, standing all straight like a toy soldier.'

'Yes but Manon,' I asked, 'what did she do?'

'Her parents died not long after the war started and she went and joined up as a nurse or something, went to Flanders. I sort of remember she was very kind to my mam when she heard about Rob. Came and talked to her when she was back on leave. She was very quiet, but very sad. The listening sort.'

Mrs Jones stared at Dawn again, who recoiled slightly. 'The house subsided while she was away. All sorts of shafts all over the place up here. Maybe it was the one that caused all the trouble. Anyway, she gave orders for it to be knocked down and had a small house built there instead. That'll be yours I suppose.' Dawn nodded, though I knew she didn't know whether it was or not. It must have seemed to be the safest response. 'She never lived in it though. She died in Flanders. You never hear about the nurses who died. Just the soldiers. But she'd left instructions to bring her locket back and bury it in her garden. Don't suppose you ever found it did you love?'

Dawn shook her head.

'Mrs Jones,' she said hesitantly, 'why did you say Manon was looking out of me a moment ago.'

'Don't be silly love, why would I say something like that?'

Dawn exchanged a glance with me and went on, 'sometimes I see a ghost crying in the garden. Do you think it's Manon looking for her locket?'

Mrs Jones snorted and poured us some more weak squash. 'Don't believe in ghosts.' she announced firmly, 'against the Bible that is. Mind,' she went on thoughtfully, 'it wouldn't be the locket she was looking for, it would be the tunnel. The one that caused all the trouble.'

Sue had gone back to eye-rolling. She hadn't any patience for this sort of thing. 'What trouble, Mrs Jones? What tunnel? Only I've got to be back for tea soon.'

The old lady was silent, staring at her long dead brother, fuzzy in a dog eared photograph. I worried she was going out to blur again herself. Then she sighed and shook herself slightly.

'Well it was before I was born, but it was a bit of a scandal. They say she fell in love with a poor boy from down the hill. They say there was an old tunnel between the house on the hill and the works by the river, really old mind, from way back. Some say slaves dug it for the Romans, who knows? Anyway, they say Manon used to sneak out of bed and go down the tunnel to meet him and then her Dad found out and finish.'

'Finish?' said Sue, startled.

'Her dad put a stop to it, see. Sealed up the entrance to the tunnel and then pretty much kept Manon under lock and key. All she got was chapel, walks with her mother, home. Poor girl.'

'And the boy?' I asked, 'what happened to him?'

'Ran away. "Not much of a man if he didn't fight for her" they said.' She smiled her vague old lady smile at Dawn, and then frowned, pulling her head back as if trying to focus, 'Manon? What you doing looking out of this one? You won't find that tunnel up by here. He's not coming back. Give up, girl.'

We quickly said goodbye and left. The spring evening was cold and we put the shivering down to that. Sue said she had to get home and left us, but I walked Dawn home, she was close to tears.

'Do you think I'm possessed?' She said after a while.

'Of course not, don't be silly. She's just getting lots of things muddled up. Half the time she cooks tea for Mr Jones even though he's been dead for five years.' I hooked my arm into hers, 'Don't worry.

How can she even remember what Manon looked like? It was sixty years ago. She's just muddling Manon in the big house with you in the house Manon built after. But tell you what, maybe on Saturday we'll see if we can find the locket. Your parents won't mind if we do some digging.'

'No, it's all right,' Dawn shook her head and smiled weakly, 'let's leave it.'

Not long after that, Mrs Jones nearly burnt her house down leaving something under the grill and her son got her put in a home. We got our project in and got good marks, partly because of Dawn's notes and partly because of the really melodramatic story she wrote about Manon being deserted by her lover and weeping over the photograph in her locket on the battlefields of Flanders.

Soon after that, we grew up a bit more and even Dawn started to get pop music and want to wear make-up and when we sat round in the dark to share ghost stories, they were always more hair-raising than a depressed woman dripping round a garden because she'd never had the guts to stand up to her parents. Then a few more years passed, boys, exams, parties, leaving home, drifting apart, getting married. And one by one our parents moved away or died or both and the last links with each other were gone completely.

Last thing I expected to see when I was trailing the news websites on a spring Sunday was the name of that obscure village whose dust I shook off all those years ago. Back then it was a place so small that there were only ten children outside running about, cycling, playing ball, what have you all the time and a bus every two hours. What must it be like now?

'Mysterious steps appear in rural garden' ran the headline. '"We thought the pergola was subsiding slightly," said the shocked owners, "and the next morning it had collapsed and there was this hole in the ground and we could see stone steps leading down. We never knew anything about it. And we paid for a full survey and everything."'

I found the local news page and followed the story for as long as there was nothing more exciting happening. Somehow they persuaded the owners to have a proper dig on the site and they opened up the hole to find it led into a tunnel boring down into the hillside. If the hole had opened up back in Dawn's garden when we were twelve, we've been down it like rabbits before the earth had settled, but nowadays it was a whole week before a bunch of archaeologists with safety equipment were given the go-ahead to find out what was at the other end.

And at the other end they found a sealed exit and the skeleton of a young man.

The owners weren't putting up with that sort of thing, even though the remains were well over a hundred years old. They put the house on the market, leaving it vacate while they argued with insurers.

Out of sheer curiosity, I got a room in a local hotel and arranged a viewing. It was late evening when I got there and found that the apologetic estate agent had made a double booking. I shrugged and said I didn't mind, without mentioning the fact that I had no intention of buying. Upstairs I found the other potential vendor, a tall middle aged woman. She was standing in what had once been Dawn's room, looking out of the window into the garden and down onto where the entrance to the tunnel was, secured but not sealed. She turned and smiled at me in that hesitant way she'd always had, although now it had a little more confidence behind it.

'Hello Dawn!' I said, though perhaps I shouldn't have been surprised.

'Hello,' she replied, 'wondered if you'd turn up. I don't suppose Sue will.'

'No, it wouldn't be her thing.' I went to join her at the window. 'I wonder if they'll ever find the locket?'

'They can't,' Dawn answered pulling something out from her jacket pocket. 'I found it all those years ago. Had it ever since.'

She opened it and we looked at the two young people inside in their old fashioned clothes, hopeful. The photos separated by the hinge as the lovers had been by class and then death.

'She's gone you know.' said Dawn, looking back out again, 'I suppose she's at peace now. Manon I mean. A shame really, I'm going to buy this house and move back. It won't seem the same without her.'

TAKING SHELTER

It was Ryan who spotted her first. Stebbins was too busy fussing over the mud on his trainers where he'd slipped. It wasn't that he was cared about the work to clean them, it was more the worry that his mother wouldn't do a good enough job and then they wouldn't be cool anymore and that he'd have the hassle of nagging her into buying him replacements. And he was bothered about where the sodden leaves had soaked into the front of his jeans at the entrance to the cave which made him look as if he'd wet himself. The other kids would never let him forget it if they saw and it might not be so easy to keep them in line.

Ryan prodded him and Stebbins went to slap him one. Then he suddenly realised he could hear breathing from the back of the cave and see a dull glimmer of light casting shadows on the low ceiling.

'Hello lads,' came a female voice. Stebbins couldn't make out whether it was a nice voice or not. There was a mellowness there but also a harshness and a coldness and a sense of desolation. Her words were thick with age and the effort to haul the English out of her memory. It reminded him of his great grandmother, that daft old bat, who'd forgotten how to speak English and was locked in her own world now, wittering away to long dead siblings. No-one in the family could speak Welsh and some of the carers in the care home couldn't even speak much English.

'What you staring at?' snarled Stebbins. She was unnerving him, but he wouldn't let her see it.

'I'm staring at you,' said the woman firmly. The light increased but he couldn't see where it was coming from. It seemed to emanate from her face itself and yet it flickered. One moment she seemed young and smooth, with thick curls and full bright lips and then she seemed old and wrinkled and haggard with thin locks flying and tangling around her and then she seemed blue and then white as if filled with electricity - the bones showing through her skin.

Stebbins swallowed and he could sense Ryan trembling like a puppy.

'Stop it,' Stebbins whispered, 'don't let her get to you, she's just some mad old cow.'

'Am I then?' the woman's voice crashed through them like an explosion. 'Old I am. Mad I'm not. Cow I'm not. I belong to this place. I would not insult me, if I were you.'

The boys looked at her, trying not to huddle together in fear, trying to retreat towards the front of the cave. She hadn't moved, just flickered slightly, her hands moving... on what? Stebbins risked looking down and saw them fiddling with a sack, tying and untying strings. One young fresh hand, one old dried up hand.

'I am the Weather Witch.' she said, 'The rain that brought you in to shelter, I made that happen. Apologise to me.'

Now Stebbins snorted with laughter. 'Yeah right, of course you did. No-one makes weather but you're a witch all right, a stupid old witch.'

'Don't believe me boy?' the woman said calmly.

She untied one of the strings and loosened the bag slightly. The wind outside increased slightly, the rain fell heavier.

'Supposed to impress us is it?' smirked Stebbins, 'That's just luck. It's what it does here. Wind, rain, more rain, it's February. It's what it does.'

She tied the string again and untied another, the rain stopped and the sun blazed down so that the wet winter ground steamed. She fiddled again and there was a sudden clap of thunder and lightning struck the entrance to the cave inches from the boys' feet. Then the rain returned.

'Fluke.' Stebbins said, less certainly. 'You can't frighten us.' It wasn't true.

Ryan was crying. 'Say sorry,' he urged, 'just say sorry.'

'Mad old witch, mad old cow' Stebbins repeated louder, 'I'm gonna find out where you live and I'm gonna make your life hell!'

The light in the woman dimmed. Her breath came slow and thick.

'Oh lads,' she said softly, 'here is where I live. And do you know, I have an urge for some company.'

She fiddled with the strings on her bag again and shook it hard. The rain stopped and the boys making to leave were forced back by a freezing wind. The harder they pushed against it, the harder the wind forced them back into the cave. Then the snow came. Snow fell fast and heavy. Before they could do anything it had filled the entrance to the cave and they were trapped inside.

'Let us out' shouted Stebbins, hugging himself to keep warm. The air was getting colder and the snow was hardening, turning to ice.

'Too late now, boys.' said the old woman, and the overhang at the front of the cave crashed down as the ice penetrated a fault in the rock.

It made the local papers. First time the village had been famous ever.

'Lively rascals, full of mischief, always up to tricks' was how they were described. Read that how you like. The locals just wondered what they'd been doing to make the front of the cave collapse like that, and how their bodies had frozen solid in the mildest February for fifty years.

DEATH BY O.E.D

Dave was doing his best. It was murder fighting off the zombies with a chain saw. Although actually...is it murder when you're killing the undead? But he knew his duty as a member of the neighbourhood watch. Usually it was just admonishing litterers and dog-messers, but now his moment of glory had arrived. The zombies had appeared when he lifted the man hole cover in his garden to find out what was blocking the drains and with great presence of mind, he was slaying each one as it emerged with his brand new chain saw.

When there was a bit of a lull, he paused to wipe his brow and looked up to see his neighbour glaring out of her upstairs window; the one she used as a sort of study. He'd heard she did a bit of creative writing. It would have been more useful if she'd maintain her overgrown garden. Still, each to their own. Here came another zombie, its grey fingers oozing over the edge of the man hole. Dave hoisted the chainsaw once more and went into the fray.

Volume one of the Shorter Oxford English Dictionary flew out of his neighbour's window and smacked Dave solidly in the forehead. He fell. At least he was unconscious when the zombies attacked before swarming over the fence.

Back in her house, Julie the wannabe bestselling author breathed a sigh of relief. Finally, Dave had got the message and turned off his chainsaw. She looked at the blank screen of her laptop and tried to think romantic thoughts. Julie didn't like her main character Cheryl and couldn't understand why Robert (pronounced à la française) would fall in love with her. It was shame Robert wasn't real. She quite fancied him herself. She couldn't imagine him leaving her on Saturday with two internet obsessed teenagers to go and watch a football match. Robert would be taking her out for a run in his sports car to a five course meal and an afternoon of …. anyway, she needed to get on and make him fall in love with Cheryl instead. Sigh.

Forcing soppy thoughts into her head and trying to dredge up long forgotten romantic dialogue from the dim, pre-teenage offspring past, Julie didn't register the sound of the back door opening. She vaguely heard the slow shuffling thumps of feet on the stairs, and incomprehensible moaning, but presumed her children were communicating with each other and that there would shortly be some kind of quarrel to referee. Double sigh.

The undead clambered up the stairs and separated to take on the teenagers' bedrooms. They pushed open the doors with their rotting fingers and peered inside. Two almost immobile young people lolled about looking barely conscious. Dribble was coming from one of them as she lay on the bed, earplugs shoved half a mile into each ear. The other one was staring intently at a flickering screen and twitching slightly. These two had clearly been turned into zombies already. But there must be food here somewhere.

Julie was intently typing, her mind firmly in the south of France. Robert was whispering into Cheryl's ears and Cheryl was melting. Julie didn't notice the door slowly opening.….

THE FAMILIAR

The way I see it is this. If people spent more time looking with open minds and less time looking to find fault, they might be happier. They might actually find what they're looking for.

See, those people down there, yeah those ones - the ones with the flaming torches. They're looking for evil and they've decided what it looks like (which is a simple formula to them. 'Different = Dangerous') and so they've found something that sorta fits the bill, ignored anything that don't and are acting on their assumptions. Plus you can guarantee a bloke down the tavern said or one of the elders said or THEY said. No-one knows which bloke, which elder, which THEY. It's just got to be true. Cos the minute you say 'whoa - hang on - who told you that? Where's the proof?' suspicion will fall on you. So you don't say nothing. And no-one says nothing and before you know it everyone's got caught up in the moment and one set (a small set mind) is handing out flaming torches like they're toffee apples and everyone just takes one cos they don't know what else to do. What are they? Ants? Bees? Sheep?

People say they're the top of creation and look at them: hardly an individual amongst them, unless you count that poor wretch in the middle. She couldn't get more individual, could she, bless her. That's one woman who asked 'why' too many times. 'Why don't we try this?' 'Why do we always do it that way?' 'Why don't you just be yourself and stop worrying what other people think?' That's what got her where she is now.

And see the people round the edges, yeah, I know, the smoke's getting a bit thick. If you're bothered now, best not stick around. But look: the ones that are hanging back, the ones that are thinking 'why am I holding this torch?' 'why is this a good idea?' 'why do we think this will make things better?' Yes those ones - they'll be next, mark my words. They're gonna have to think quick if they don't want to do the thing but also don't want the others to know they didn't.

Cos the thing is, people do think 'Why?' But they think it the wrong way. They think 'Why did the harvest fail again? Why is my cow barren? Why did my child die?' and then they look around and find someone to punish for it. Life's short. Who can blame them you might say. But funny how no-one says 'why's the harvest been so good? Why have I got more calves than I can sell? Why is my child so strong and healthy its face glows like an apple?' and then find someone to praise for it. That woman - what did she ever do? She wasn't perfect. Who is? But you gonna say that one little woman is guilty of everything that's gone wrong - this year's rain, this year's non-stop rain, the cold, the crops rotting in the fields, the blue babies? You think they gonna say to their maker when they meet him - 'oh that little woman - we thought she was bigger than you'? Nah - nor me pal. If someone could put that to them ... see the folk on the outside, they're asking themselves that right now and trying to fade off into the night - look that one's put his torch out, that one is starting to cry a little. But most of the rest ... I reckon now their blood is up now. If a voice came from Heaven they wouldn't hear it or they'd blame the poor wretch herself for conjuring it up. See they've looked for me too but they won't find me. I'll miss her, but there's nothing I can do to help now. Most respect I can show is by going away and not watching what they do to her. Best I can do is find someone else like her. Someone who don't mind a companion that's been battered by life and shows it but don't think it's the mark of the devil or nothing. Someone who knows how to ask 'Why?' the right way.

But you and me, mate, we're lucky cos we don't waste time with talk. We may think 'Why's there no food? Why can't I find somewhere warm and dry to sleep? Why is the only thing caressing me a pile of fleas?' but we don't go and blame anyone. We think 'there was food once - there'll be food again. There will be shelter somewhere one day, there will be caress sometime.' And if not, well, that's life innit? Us and them and the fleas and the sun coming up and the rain coming or not coming and birth and death and the whole shebang - it's all life.

Come on, best stick with me mate. No point asking why this happened. It'll happen till the end of time or until people stop looking to blame others and start looking inside themselves and learn to just accept the fleas along with the caresses. They're lighting the pyre now.

Let's go. Don't look back. The sun always comes up. It always comes up.

RETURN

Without the map she would not have come. The map felt weaker than her own resolve and polluted by her adult state. Forty years had passed and she was settled a hundred miles away. She had long closed the drawer on that part of her life, packing up and disposing of more than books and diaries. But the map had survived several culls of possessions by her parents as their homes shrank and then by her widowed mother moving to a sheltered flat. Unfolding its feeble creases had caused tears to drip onto the faded biro and felt tip. She cried for the child she had been and the stranger she now was.

And so, here she stood, at the edge of the copse, beyond the house in which the sweet-munching spoilt boy with black rotten teeth had lived; beyond the collapse of corrugated iron which had been a pig pen; beyond the tree she and Ffion had climbed to hide from their little sisters; beyond the bracken where they played cowboys and indians; beyond the blank nettly, brambly space where the playground had been, where the teenagers had mocked their attempts to touch the sky on the swings; beyond the rocks they'd climbed and from which, alone again, she had sometimes sat and stared at the mountain on the other side of the river, a greenish mound like a giant settled for a sleep.

Forty-two years ago Ffion had swung on the gate, claimed her friendship and taught her to climb trees. Recently Ffion emailed 'don't go back' but she had come anyway.

Without the map she would not have come. She ought to have been afraid. Night was falling. But how could she be afraid? Modern bad boys were warm indoors playing games online, too engrossed to be out bullying or vandalising.

The trees were still as imperious. From underneath, you looked up and they looked black and cold against the sky. One of them had once had rope dangling from a high branch. Someone back then told her that one of the more stupid bad boys, messing about, had nearly hanged himself. Now she wouldn't be surprised to see the rope still there, had never shaken the imagined image of the struggling child and his brothers frantically running for help. She remembered that boy setting his dog on her cat and the cat slashing the terrier's face. She imagined that boy now, fat and middle aged, and wondered if he ever recalled the strange, old fashioned English girl from the house opposite the lane to the woods.

Now she settled down on the three slabs of rock which fell together in a box like a chest or a tomb or a portal under the tallest tree. It would have been knee deep in bluebells back then, a blue haze under the black larches. She wondered if bluebells still grew here, could still struggle up through the undergrowth. Who had kept it all clear when they were children? She had assumed, still assumed, the wood to be self-cleansing; the balance of nature stopping any one species taking over. The bracken high where the trees had been sparse, green and curled in spring and tinder arson-tempting dry in summer; under the dense dark trees, pine needles and thick rich silky grass.

She had trusted only one friend with her secret: that in her loneliest days, strange and out of synch, transplanted from rural Berkshire to West Glamorgan, mocked for her accent, uncomprehending of theirs, she had gone alone to the river and alone to the copse and had talked to the spirits there and they had comforted her. They had sparkled under the trees hanging over the tumbling river and they had murmured from the larches and she had felt at peace.

Life was not so lonely anymore. But it was busy. No longer any time to just sit. Constant rushing and organising, her ears buzzing with demands and responsibilities. Once she had been the lonely girl who drew a map to show where the fairies were, not the sparkling babyish tutu-wearing dolls, but the living breathing spirits of wood and water. Now she was a practical adult, sensible and unemotional. Or that was what people thought. Life had taught her to hide herself.

But here she was, sitting under the trees as the full moon rose. She closed her eyes and was silent. But the wood was not silent. The air was cold, but she was not cold. The tree felt warm to her back and her heart filled with peace. 'Croeso,' whispered the air. 'We're glad to see you happy now' it breathed.

She opened her eyes and saw a child before her. Silver and made of moonlight and holding something and then gone. And she remembered. It had been what she had meant to do all those years ago. She unfolded the map for the last time - she could barely see it in the dark but she knew that it set out all the secret magical places and did not belong to her anymore.

She folded it back up and poked it down into a cavity under the tree. 'Diolch,' she heard.

She stood up and rolled her shoulders and looked up into the moonlit trees. 'I'm going now' she said, 'I won't be back again. But I want to say thank you. Thank you for being my friend when I was so lonely. Thank you for helping me learn to be happy on my own. Thank you for reminding me how to listen.'

She walked away, down past where the playground had been, where the pigsty had been, where the boy with the rotten teeth had lived and got in her car, parked outside her old house. She looked up at the moon as she drove away - she would never come back. But she was taking the child she had once been away with her and together they would learn to be still.

GOTH GIRL

Chocolate box the relations called it. They had rented for a while, a relatively modern house in the middle of the village; but their aim had always been to buy somewhere with character. When the cottage came up, they couldn't believe there was so little competition.

None of the locals would buy it. In the Post Office, an older woman said to her 'Granny Davison always said it was a strange place and she lived there her whole adult life.'

Emily looked at her waiting for something more. She wondered if the word 'Granny' was being used as the old country euphemism for witch.

As if reading her mind, the other woman thinned her lips and said 'Granny Davison was my grandmother on my father's side' and turned to get her pension.

Emily and Tom loved it. Locals exchanged glances. Other incomers drew in their breath and wondered about the cost of insuring the thatch, the cost of replacing the thatch, mice in the thatch, woodworm in the beams, the lack of double glazing and central heating, the dark low windowed rooms. But Emily and Tom stood on the threshold and unlocked the door with a thrill of anticipation.

The house stood at the side of what had once been a main road to the cathedral town, but was now a back road, serviced by a twice daily bus which wound through all the lanes picking up a handful of passengers from outlying hamlets. To the side of the house a narrow lane fell down into a hollow where two other cottages sat and opposite, an even narrower lane headed up a hill to nowhere. At the back was a small extension which had been built long before modern planning and conservation laws which Emily could kit out as a studio.

They entered the house full of hope. Tom's new job was what he had always wanted, Emily had exactly the right number of contracts and she was hugging in her secret knowledge, the knowledge that she hadn't shared with Tom yet. When he was at work, Emily sat in the studio working on her illustrations but from time to time, when she was pausing with a cup of tea, she would look out at the chaotic, pretty, sunlight dappled garden and gently stroke her still flat stomach, whispering 'hang on in there, hang on.' It was the latest she had ever been.

When she wasn't working, Emily was redecorating the house in unapologetic modern colours, brightening up the Elizabethan corners with vibrant blues and reds and golds. Working upstairs, she would often spot one of the teenagers waiting for the bus on the other side of the road; an indecisive looking girl. She would sit down on the old road marker one minute, then stand up, then wander a few steps and then sit down again. Her impatience was almost palpable. She was dressed in sort of vague goth style, her clothes long, dark and a little dusty. Her hair was long and a little tangled. The bus would come, stop, deposit Emily's neighbour and drive off, leaving the road marker empty.

Emily knew it was over before the blood came. She recognised the cramps but they were worse than usual, dragging, draining, making her nauseous. She knew there was nothing she could do. She did her best to collect the blood, to see if there was anything to be seen of this almost child, but it was impossible to discern. Crying silently, she wrapped the blood up in a piece of bright silk from her fabric store and buried it in the garden. Impossible to flush her hope away as if it was waste.

Blindly Emily went out of the front of the house and through the gate stood in the treacherous sunshine, looking up as if there was somewhere to escape. Turning, she saw the goth girl staring at her. Something in the girl's face made Emily feel that her mind was being read. The girl stood up and started towards her. Emily could see tears in her eyes. But the bus was coming. For a moment, she thought the girl might not get onto the bus and half wanted her to stay and half wished she wouldn't, but the bus came and went and the girl had gone.

Time passes. The edges of the wound starts to knit. Hope creeps back in stockinged feet. With winter came heavy frosts and heavy rain, one after the other for weeks and weeks. Potholes appeared in the road outside their house and when it became impassable, the council finally did something about it. Goth girl was sometimes still waiting for the bus, even though it couldn't get through. The council tried to get away with the minimum repair but the road started to collapse and a proper job was necessary. It was then that the bones were found. Ancient bones, a slender body curled defensively. The police were called, although, if crime had been committed, the perpetrators had been dead for 500 years. The vicar was called and accepted a cup of coffee from Emily and Tom, watching from the sidelines. 'Suicide probably, they used to bury them at cross-roads so that their spirit wouldn't be able to work out which way to go and therefore couldn't haunt anyone. She'll get a proper burial now, bless her.'

A few days later, Tom noticed that the frost had also damaged the threshold - the old piece of stone had a crack in it. Uncertain whether this would destabilise the house, but certain it would destabilise the porch, he arranged for builders to come. Lifting the stone, they found another curled pile of bones. Old crumbly bones. A baby. Again the police pointlessly reported it to the coroner. Again, the vicar came and surveyed the little grave. 'The other thing they used to do when they built houses. Sometimes it was a cat, sometimes an unbaptised baby - buried under the threshold and supposed to ward off evil. They were strange, unpleasant, superstitious times.'

'It was hers.' said Emily.

'Whose?' asked the vicar.

'The girl from the cross roads - I know it was.'

'Could be,' said the vicar. 'We can bury them together, they'll be company for each other.'

The double burial took place on a weekday morning. Other things in local news were more interesting, so it was a lonely occasion, with only a few people to witness it. There were no names to give those two rejected souls but Emily laid flowers on the unmarked grave and told the vicar she would pay for a headstone.

It was a few days before Emily realised that goth girl had stopped sitting on the road marker, even though the bus had started running again and then one day, standing outside the front soaking up the spring sunshine, she saw her coming up the road from the village. She had never seen her walk so far. The girl looked just as raggedy but walked with more confidence and a slight smile on her face. She had a shawl round her and as she came closer, Emily realised that the shawl held a tiny baby, its little hand just visible above the edge of the shawl. The girl walked up the gate, entered and walked straight past Emily through the house to the garden. Startled, Emily followed and saw the girl kneel by the spot in the garden where the little piece of bloody silk had been buried. The girl turned briefly to Emily and smiled. She planted a sprig of rosemary in the soil and rising, shifted the infant in her shawl, walked back through the house and down the hill, her form now clear, then fading, then gone.

OVER THE BRIDGE

It's a slow amble down the slope and the railings on either side are a little wonky. One set appears to be held up by brambles and on the other side, bordering the big green field with the sad horse tethered in his brown circle, the railings slope idly as if no-one ever told them to stand up straight. They were painted black once, but now they're dull rust colour. You can taste the iron just by looking at them. Right at the end, just before the bridge the bars have been bent apart so that someone small can squeeze through.

The start of the bridge is overhung with trees of course, the same trees which overhang the river on both sides. The railings of the bridge are still black, mostly, and the paint is smooth and lumpy under my hands as I look over.

Upstream, the river curves away but the depths still sparkle under the trees and little droplets of light and dust shine and spin and dart - appearing and disappearing. The water is darkest as it disappears around the bend but the spots of sunshine on the waves and in the air make it friendly and welcoming. I want to speak to the flashes of brightness but find I am dumb.

Turning, I look over the other side of the bridge. You can see further downstream and it is not so overhung. For a few metres, the water runs swiftly, weed straggling with the flow. Deceptively it plays over hidden deeps and stony shallows as if it will not speed up and deepen as it bends away, as it nears the waterfall at the other end, before it pours out into the bigger river and on to the sea.

The black bars of the bridge are hot under my hands, even under the trees and when I stand on the bottom row with my feet between the balusters to lean over, the metal is hot on my toes as well.

Just out from under the bridge is a small sandbank, dry enough to stand on. A little girl is there alone crouched down, intently staring at something. She is around nine I guess and her feet in white sandals are planted firmly on the edge of the lapping water. Her cotton dress is short and floral and her brown hair is clipped back from a face which is turned from me. She is carefully picking out stones and examining them. A little pile has built up and I can see that some are smooth and pretty and some are like black glass, jagged and sparkly. After a while, she stops picking out stones and just hunches, elbows on her knees, chin on her hands, staring into the water. It is shallow enough here for her to make out all the little lives going about their business in the lee of the main flow. Sometimes, she looks up and downstream and then returns to her observations or her foraging.

If she has any doubts and fears, it seems they are forgotten. Now she appears totally content and safe and full of hope and peacefully alone.

In a while, she will go home, taking some of her finds; she will say goodbye to the river and the sparkling lights who listen to her secrets and her worries; she will take one last look at the nymph, busily marching round its underwater kingdom and hope that she will be there when it emerges and transforms.

I look at her and wish I could remember the words the river understands, wish I knew how to find the pretty stones, still feel sad that the next time she comes the nymph will be gone and a myriad dragon-flies will fly around but none will recognise her.

If she looks up, she will not see me because I do not exist yet. She will see nothing but a bridge, going home in one direction and going away from home in another.

She will grow up and stop visiting the sand bank. Some of her worries will come true and others won't. She will forget how to talk to the wild, but the wild will not forget how to speak to her.

The river will flow on, the waterfall will carry her away, the big river will swallow her up, the sea will engulf her, but she will be all right. In the end, she will be all right. The light sparkling under the trees will bring her home.

IN THE OLIVE GROVE

There are sisters and sisters.

Marta was the good girl and no-one ever noticed her except to tell her what she was doing wrong. Doing things right was the expectation. Marta was the oil in the machine of life, keeping things going, people fed and clothed. She knew where things were or might be or should be. She remembered special occasions. She wiped tears and held hands and gave advice when asked and tried not to mind when the advice was ignored. If she got angry or miserable, she was accused of moodiness. It disturbed people when the machine didn't run properly. No-one ever said 'you look tired or sad or lonely.' They just told her to pull herself together and stop being selfish. So Marta just got on with things. When she had been little, she used to lie out in the sun and watch the clouds or the sun playing through the leaves of the olive trees. Now she was always looking down - into the basin, into the fire, onto the floor.

Miryam on the other hand was fun. She could be scatterbrained and she could be untidy. She sang and laughed and cried and shouted in equal measure but no-one minded. If Marta was the oil in the machine of life, Miryam was the decoration on the machine and the spice in the sauce. People thanked her when did her duties, and excused her when she didn't. Miryam was grown up yet still sat about outside whenever she could, grinding the wheat and singing, or just singing; taking her temper out on the laundry; playing tag with the children. Even when she was looking down, she restlessly wondered where the answers were. If Marta sat on her own, chances are she'd stay that way. If Miryam sat on her own, people swarmed round her. It was as if the light inside her warmed them up and just her presence brought them to life. Sometimes she wished that they would all leave her alone and stop trying to drain the energy out of her.

On the Sabbath, when she was not allowed to cook or clean or sew, Marta sat with the other women and watched them. Miryam as usual was talking nineteen to the dozen to her friends, playing hide and seek with their babies. Marta wondered whether there was anything in Miryam's head except silliness, if she ever thought a deep thought or pondered the heavens or worried about the future. Marta looked at the babies and small children and felt the ache in her spread from her empty womb to clasp her throat. She could feel her face hardening into a grimace, her lips thinning against the sob and her eyes stung. How could you grieve for something you had never had? But she felt a longing for a child even stronger than the longing for her dead parents whom she'd loved so much. Didn't Miryam feel like that too? What if they never married? What if their lot was to stay with Eleazar until they wizened away? Marta longed for the Sabbath to be over so that she could get back to work and drive her sadness out with the dust on the floor.

Using her veil, Miryam hid her face from Adina's baby and then peeped out feigning surprise. The baby gurgled in delight. There was no sound like it. Adina handed the child over to rest her arms and Miryam smelled the milky scent of his curly head. She wondered what she would call her own. Things would work out somehow. She looked over to Marta and watched her face closing down. Who knew what was going on in her head, but she'd be snapping at them all later. Miryam wished Marta would just smile a bit more. She wished they found time to wander about like they had when they were little, hiding from the chores in the olive grove, making up stories, lying hand in hand on the wild thyme staring up at the sky in companionable silence, wondering if there was more to life than growing up, marrying, having children, working, working, working and then dying. Miryam longed for the Sabbath to be over so that she didn't have to sit still so much and think. What if people stopped liking her? What if she got miserable like Marta? What if this was all there was to life?

The following day Eleazar's friend came to visit. Marta woke early and started to work, anger building and building. She turned over conversations in her head. Over and over: why am I the only one doing this? What would you do if I wasn't here? I feel like running away. Where to? Where to? There was so much to do. Food to prepare and then clear away, the house looked untidy or maybe not untidy, but boring and drab. Marta moved things about and rearranged pots. She started work on the feast and put the bread to rise.

Miryam got up and started putting things back to where they'd been before and Marta snapped at her. Miryam rolled her eyes and walked out to get some water. Clearly she wasn't going to be able to do anything right today.

By the time she'd got back, the friend had arrived and was sitting outside with Eleazar. They were talking. Talking about worry. Miryam slowed down and leant against the doorway, the water jar against her hip. Here was Eleazar pouring his heart out, how hard it had been to manage when their father died, how much he wanted his sisters to marry decent men, how much he wanted a loving wife of his own. He paused and spoke more quietly, more hesitantly: how he worried about what would happen if he died young, died before he'd found husbands for Marta and Miryam.

She had never thought about whether Eleazar worried, he was the calm, sensible one. Not brooding over fury like Marta, not stamping like herself, but just sitting quiet.

The friend listened, scribbling in the dust with a stick, waited till Eleazar went quiet and spoke gently. 'Take your worry to God. He cares about you. Imagine you are a child with a broken toy, wouldn't you take it to your loving father to mend and then stop fretting because you know that he will fix it for you?'

Miryam looked closely at her brother. She could see the thoughts fighting for words which he was afraid to express: 'but He let our parents die, He left us to struggle, it must be something we're doing wrong, He's left us to sort it out ourselves.'

In the end, Eleazar simply said: 'some toys can't be fixed.'

'That's true' his friend answered, 'sometimes you have to let go and let your father comfort you. But you have to go to him for that comfort. He cannot force it on you.'

Inside the house, Marta was banging things about. This meant that she was angry and fed up of working on her own. Miryam hesitated then put the water jar down and sat by her brother's feet. She cleared her throat and said 'They say we must do more sacrifices to please God but it seems nothing we can do is enough.'

She thought he would look angry at being addressed by a woman, but he just smiled reassuringly, 'Sacrifice is not required, it is a matter of faith. Trusting that in the end, everything will make a sense you cannot now see; looking to Him for comfort rather than to yourself for a solution.'

'How can we..' she started but Marta had appeared at the door, nearly crying from frustration.

'Teacher,' Marta stammered, 'I am working all alone and my sister isn't helping me. There is so much to do, so many of you to feed.' Her lip was trembling. 'I can't do it anymore. I am...'

The friend gestured to her to sit down next to Miryam and finished her sentence 'You are at the end of yourself?'

Marta nodded and put her head in her hands. Miryam reached out to gently touch her, whispering, 'I'm sorry, I just want to listen some more.' But Marta pulled away and started to go inside.

'No' the friend said firmly, 'you must be still. You must all be still.'

More gently, he said, 'Sit down Marta. Sit back Eleazar. Just be still for a little while. Don't be afraid of the silence, of the sound of your heart. Let your thoughts stop. Listen. Worrying changes nothing. It just boils your mind.'

The meal was over, the friend had gone and the sisters had cleared up. Eleazar had gone to sit with the other men of the village. The afternoon was hot and the house was cool. Marta restlessly moved about in the shade, rearranging things again, wondering what job to start next, weaving or grinding or preparing the evening meal. She looked up and saw Miryam watching her with and smiled. Little sister. When did we stop being friends?

'Let's leave it,' she said after a moment, 'come and lie under the olives like we used to. It would be nice to be still for a while.'

SWEET SIXTEEN

In Rose's town a girl had three options if she lived to sixteen. She got married or she ran away dressed up as a boy to join the army or she got fed to the dragon. Some of the naughtier (or wiser) girls made sure they escaped the dragon by losing the main qualifying credential for being dragon fodder before they hit sixteen. But they didn't subsequently escape marriage when their fathers found out.

Boys got a couple more years on the girls and no-one considered feeding them to the dragon. Boys got to wait a bit before marriage and some ran away to join the army. Some even came back again; the nasty boys nastier, the quiet boys quieter, the imaginative boys traumatised.

Two days before her birthday, Rose considered her options. Marriage was out. The town boys were dreary or nasty or just eyed her as if she was a prize cow, estimating her breeding potential. They smirked at her bosom, bursting out over the top of her blouse but frowned at her otherwise petite and narrow frame, wondering if she had the hips for child-bearing under her petticoats. They would have tried to find out but she wasn't the sort. Not one of them thought maybe she didn't want to force out baby after baby until she went mad or died. They seemed to think it was their duty to knock that book reading nonsense out of her and give her a proper woman's job. Nope, she wasn't ready for that. She quite fancied learning under the midwife but her parents had vetoed that one. The income was good but the prospects poor. Things went wrong, the midwife job title tended to change to witch and the expression 'being fired' had a whole new meaning.

Running away to join the army didn't appeal. For a start, she didn't like killing things, let alone people and secondly, she thought she'd look stupid in breeches and thirdly, she never thought she'd be able to strap her bosom down enough to pass as a boy. Besides, without a horse or a disguise, she'd never be able to get away over the mountains.

So dragon it was then. If that's the way it was going to be, might as well get eaten as soon as possible. No point in having a birthday party, cake, candles, the pretty dress, the flowers in the hair just to get munched up as the sun went down.

Rose climbed the side of the mountain which led up to the dragon's lair. He was quite an accommodating dragon, didn't really bother them too much. In lean years when there weren't many sixteen year old girls to keep him full, he settled for sheep and pigs and generally kept himself to himself. Occasionally he accidentally started fires on the mountain side when the heather got dry, but otherwise he was quite a relaxing presence: crooning away over his treasure, theoretically ready to defend them in the face of an attack; though quite who would hike all the way up here to attack and for what, had never been established.

Rose sat down neatly on a blackened bit of rock and looked into the edge of the cave. She could just make out the dragon's scaly snout, little puffs of smoke wafting gently up when he breathed out.

'Er hello, dragon,' she called.

The dragon peered out at her and looked puzzled.

'I thought I'd come early, it's a while since you ate Amelia, I thought you might be hungry. I thought I'd get it over with.'

The dragon spoke to her. Unfortunately it was in Dragonese, which no-one understood and Rose shrugged, trying to look like something you'd want to eat quickly without too much munching. Like a canapé.

A behind her voice made her jump: 'He says, you're not sixteen until Tuesday.'

She turned to find a boy sitting on one of the other rocks. He was about eighteen with messy blond hair and those things on his face over his eyes, the things that helped you see. He had a book on his lap and was writing in it with a bit of charcoal. Despite the fact that she didn't want to get married and was about to offer herself as a virgin sacrifice, Rose couldn't help sitting up straighter and trying to look intelligent. It was rare to find a boy with a book. Even rarer to find one who looked attractive, if in a short sighted vague sort of way. A sturdy but nervous looking pony was tied to a burnt looking tree a few feet away, out of sight of the dragon.

'I know, but well, why wait? I'm not going to exactly enjoy the party leading up to being munched or crunched or swallowed or whatever he does. What does he do? Can you ask him?'

The boy spoke to the dragon. The dragon replied at length, rolled his eyes and put his head back on the ground as if in deep depression.

'The dragon says, actually, it sort of depends on the girl. Mostly they're too scrawny and young to have any flavour. He says you're one like that - you'd get swallowed whole, although he might dip you in chillies first. He says not to worry, he'll asphyxiate you with carbon monoxide first, so you won't know a thing. He says mostly, he wishes they'd stop feeding him young girls and feed him some of the nice fat mature specimens they have down in the village, starting with the Lady of the Manor and the Burgomaster. He says he doesn't think you'd miss them, and they'd have a bit of flavour.'

Rose thought briefly and wickedly of the revolting burgomaster with his groping tendencies and the vicious old cow at the castle for whom nothing was ever good enough. She visualised them roasting on a spit before being chewed slowly by the dragon, fat dripping down his jowls. That was terrible. What a terrible thing to think. She shook the image out of her head.

'Who are you anyway and what are you doing?'

The boy, who was sketching in his book, looked up and blushed. She realised he'd been sketching her. She went over and saw a simple but perfect likeness of a young girl with untidy plaits and a slightly defiant face. It wasn't how she looked in the mirror, it wasn't quite how she liked to imagine herself but it was her. Last time she'd seen a picture of herself drawn by a boy it had mostly consisted of bosom.

'I'm Guy,' he said, 'I had the choice of marriage or the army, so I ran away. I didn't want to do either. I just wanted to travel and study things. I thought there must be more to the world than my little village or even our little country, wherever we are. I want to know if everywhere is like this, if all people look like us or speak like us or if they're different. If there really are dog-headed people and people with faces in their stomachs. And I want to study dragons - they're dying out. Did you know? Yours is very old. He hasn't seen another dragon in a hundred years.'

Rose looked at the dragon, huffing away in his lair. A small trickle of gold was coming over his shoulder as he shifted. He did look rather like her grandfather sleeping in his chair.

She watched as Guy flicked through his book, seeing his scrawly handwriting and neat sketches.

'Where do your folk think you've gone?' she asked.

'They think I've run away to go on the stage. They couldn't really imagine what a man who didn't like fighting could do apart from put paint on their faces and play act. Anyway, I've nearly finished here. I'm heading off at sunset.'

'Can I come too?' she said suddenly. 'I can write a lot neater than you can.'

Guy looked her over and shrugged. 'That would be helpful. I can't always read what I've written. Can you bring food and more paper?'

'Yes' she said, getting up and brushing down her skirt.

She paused as she turned to go down the hill.

'Do we have to get married and have babies?' she said.

'Er...do you want to?' he said, looking alarmed.

'No.' Another thought: 'do I have to wear breeches or strap my bosom down?'

Guy eyed her bosom and flushed: 'Only if you want but I'd keep your options open, a pony's a bit bouncy.'

'Will there be dragons?'

Guy looked at the dragon, snoozing in the sun and asked a quiet question in Dragonese. There was a sleepy response.

'He says he hopes so. He says best chance is head as far East as we can. There's this place called China. He says, tell that girl to hurry up. He says tell the townsfolk: the bottom line is forget sixteen year old girls, dragons prefer pork every time.'

RETRO

The world had ended. Or perhaps it only Susan's world which had ended. But if that wasn't bad enough, though she might have staggered on as a husk in the real world, that too seemed on the verge of destruction. It only needed the Soviet Union and Ronald Reagan to get involved in the Falklands War and all that would be left would be two red buttons.

She had talked her mother into the bleach and the perm and the bright pink polka dot dress with the short ra-ra skirt and it had made no difference at the end of term party. Andrew hadn't noticed her properly. Or maybe it was just that Tracey had upstaged her again with flirting and innuendo. To Andrew, Susan was obviously still an awkward little girl and not a woman with a heart full of love. She had been crying silently all through Friday and into Saturday and for once her father was sensitive enough to recognise heart break when he saw it and had ushered the rest of the family out on a shopping trip.

Susan sat on the seat of the telephone table in the hall just on the off chance that Andrew would realise that he'd gone off with the wrong girl at the party, find a phone box so that he could ring Susan and beg her to go out with him instead. That's if he had the necessary 2ps to ring directory enquiries and call her.

The sun slanting through the front door onto the telephone was suddenly obscured and Susan realised someone was outside. For a moment, hope flared, but then she realised that whoever it was, it wasn't Andrew. It was a girl, who was looking around in some confusion as if the doorbell wasn't blindingly obvious. Wiping her eyes, Susan opened door and asked if she could help.

The strange girl brightened up immediately and said cheerfully: 'Hi, I'm from the future and I really need your help. I'm your great grand-daughter Kezia.'

Susan stared at her and before she could stop herself said: 'Hang on, I'm only seventeen and I haven't even got a baby, I haven't even er....'

Blushing, she looked closer at the other girl. It was really odd, but actually there was something about her which felt as if she was looking into a mirror. Her eyes and mouth were the same. Otherwise, the other girl had much darker skin and was taller. Her hair was a different texture as far as Susan could tell. It didn't look naturally be straight and mousy, although right now it was a sort of bright green with sparkly bits which seemed to be turning themselves on and off. Her clothes were a sort of mishmash of every current fashion going, as if she hadn't decided whether she wanted to look like Madonna or or Kim Wilde or Lady Di.

Kezia grinned apologetically. 'Yeah about that, I guess it's a bit confusing. I looked it up and you don't have time travel yet do you?'

'Er, no' said Susan carefully, wondering how quickly she could close the door and if you could get men in white coats by dialling 999.

'Only cos like for me, I can, like, I think I've got the old fashioned terminology right: I can download an app on my mobile.'

'You can what a what on your what?'

'Oh, maybe that's a bit later. Anyway let me prove it, cos I really need your help.'

Susan snorted. 'Go on then.'

Kezia got something out of her pocket. It was very small and flat and was glowing slightly. 'Right. OK. You can't be in the same place as yourself at the same time. So… pick a day last week when you weren't here but someone else was and you think you know what they were doing. It's got to be here in this house mind you, I haven't got the latest upgrade with the teleport option.'

Susan rolled her eyes and said. 'OK, last Tuesday at 4pm. I went to Tracey's for tea. That was before… anyway, my little sister was here on her own.'

Kezia fiddled about with the flat object, stepped into the hall, grabbed Susan's arm before she could say anything and pressed a button. The world blurred like it does when you've had too many Cinzanos and then righted itself. Kezia pulled Susan back out of sight under the stairs. Outside, it was raining. They could hear the TV on in the sitting room, showing some kids' programme. Suddenly, ten year old Angie came down the stairs, tottering on Susan's high heels and pursing her lips which were plastered in Susan's best lipstick.

'I knew it!' hissed Susan, 'it's all blunt….'

Just as Angie turned to find out who had spoken, Kezia pressed something again and they were back to Saturday and a sun filled but otherwise empty house.

'I've got some more proof,' said Kezia, fiddling about with her device and showing it to Susan. On the screen was a photograph - so it must be some sort of slide viewer too. The photograph was of Susan in a graduation gown, a little older and more confident.

'So they didn't press the big red button!' Susan said.

'Didn't what the what?' asked Kezia in bafflement. 'Anyway, I really do need your help.'

Susan gave up. Whatever was going on, she might as well find out what this weirdo wanted. 'Go on then, how do you think I can help you?'

'I want to borrow this dress.' said Kezia firmly, and showed her another photo on the slide viewer. It was a picture of Susan at the party on Thursday night, before Andrew went off with Tracey. She was standing still looking slightly wistful and very pale, but quite happy, her newly permed, newly bleached hair barely tamed by the white silk scarf, the pink polka dot dress close fitting and pretty to her waist and then standing out in mad frills above her knees in the pink tights and the high heeled pink stilettos.

'Why?'

'Because the 1980s are really really, what's the word... retro right now.'

'Retro?'

'Yes and I've got this party and there's this boy and I want to look really authentic and that dress is so pretty.'

Susan rolled her eyes and went and got the dress, which her mother had washed and ironed the day after its one and only outing.

'Here you go,' she said, 'I don't want it - just looking at it makes me feel miserable'. She watched as Kezia held it up to her dark skin and felt a lump coming to her throat. Whether this girl was mad or really from the future, she was going to look better in the dress than Susan had. Her legs were longer for a start.

Kezia sighed ecstatically. 'It's perfect.' she said, 'You've no idea how rare the real thing is. He's got to notice me in this.'

'Don't bank on it,' said Susan bitterly, 'it didn't work for me.'

Kezia carefully folded the pink dress over her arm and started fiddling with her gadget. She looked up and grinned, 'I wouldn't be so sure' she said, 'It was great grandpa who gave me this photo of you - he noticed you in this dress at that party and it was love at first sight. See you again in sixty years!' and she disappeared.

ICE CREAM ON MONDAY

Monday afternoon: two little girls walking down a hill in the sun. No, not a hill, a mountain. Behind us, our temporary house perched on the edge of the forest, deep dark pines climbing up over brown needles to a distant summit. The name of the mountain meant something about wild stallions. On the map, written in Welsh, the mountain had the word fforest inscribed across it. With its double-f the word had looked satisfyingly foresty. It really was a proper forest. If you stood cool under the trees you expected a wizard to appear at any moment. From our bedroom on the other side of the house, we no longer looked down on a barley field, rolling like a great golden sea like we had in our English house, but across mountainous country leading off into the mysterious unknown. And looking the other way, although we were too far inland with too many mountains in between, were seaside and beaches and sand-dunes. Dad was going to take us there at the weekend to get satisfyingly sunburnt.

When we moved to Wales, people said it would rain all the time, but it didn't. When it did rain, it was like living in a waterfall, but that was in the future. Today the sun was blazing, our feet were slippy with sweat in our white sandals. We could see across the valley to where our new house would be and there was a shimmer in the air so that it looked mysterious and magical. Between the house we were renting and the house we were buying was a river. Its name meant black, and sometimes it was black too, yet full of fairies hidden in the light sparkling on the water and dragonfly larvae to watch from a sandbank. But that was in the future too. Right now, it was another mystery to explore when we had worked up the courage and worked out the way.

So we walked down the slope, my little sister and I, looking for the ice-cream van. She was only five, a dumpling in her simple cotton dress and I had a few years left of being the taller one with longer legs. It was too hot to hold hands.

When we'd moved to Wales, English people said Welsh people would be nosey. Comparatively they were, interested instead of reserved, garrulous instead of silent. Two old ladies stopped us and asked my little sister how she was. We could barely understand them, but could grasp the intent. I flushed. I vaguely recognised them from the evening before, when Dad had made us all go to chapel. Now I had loved church back in England, it was fun, it was lively, it was full of children and it was colourful. And specifically everyone spoke English. But Dad said we should go to our local church and anyway he believed in total immersion culturalism - dive in at the deep end and you'd become one of the neighbourhood in no time. It had never worked before, but he'd never noticed. Dad was impossible to embarrass. They dressed us up in our best and took us down the steep hill to the chapel on the corner, hazy in the sun. It was full of old people. Not one other young family. Every single head, uncovered respectable male, neatly hatted female turned to look at us.

Lovely Mum was demure in her nicest summer dress, white with green polka dots. Her dark dark hair fitted her head like a cap. But she didn't have a hat.

First mistake probably. We didn't have hats either. I was wearing my loathed peach coloured dress. Plain, plain, plain. It was only a couple of shades darker than my skin. It was A line.There was nothing to make it pretty. But bookworms aren't interested in clothes are they? Boring old bookworm me in my peach dress and mousy hair. I'd tried looking soulful but just came across as sulky. Little sister meanwhile, little sister whose favourite occupations involved climbing trees and scrambling through bushes, was dolled up in an Alice in Wonderland dress lovingly made by our grandmother. She sat looking cute and sweet in her blue cotton dress and white pinafore with frilly bits, her dark hair in bunches, her big brown eyes staring round in bafflement like a puppy. Jealous? You bet ya.

So we'd sat there as the music soared with the temperature, till I could feel the sweat down my back and knew that I'd have to unpeel myself from the pew and might stand up with some varnish sticking to my legs. My fringe had glued itself to my face. Everything was in Welsh. Everything. Three years of learning to read and here I was faced with a book which might as well have been in another alphabet. The old ladies were torn between concentrating on the service, wafting their steaming faces with the hymn book and keeping an eye on this strange family in their midst. Half way through the third prayer, little sister had started to fidget. I nudged her but she got worse. I looked at her and realised her face had gone red and, slightly more strangely so had her arms. There was no time to stop her, no time to warn Mum. She let out a roar and started to cry - loud noisy sobs, big splashy tears brimming over her big brown eyes and sparkling on her eyelashes. Yes, still jealous. Nothing appealing about me when I cry - I look like a bad tempered rat who's drowned in snot.

Did I say Dad was impossible to embarrass? Well I think perhaps my little sister managed it then. We got outside with what remained of our dignity followed by two of the old ladies, clucking away at us. Oh bless her, look at her, what's the matter lovely? It was the elastic in the sleeves of her dress, it was too tight and combined with the heat, it was digging into her upper arms leaving thin ring of bloodless white and swollen agonised bulges on either side. Defeated, we had gone home.

So anyway, that was mortifying. First Sunday in a strange place and we've made our mark. Only the wrong way.

And here we are the next day looking for the ice-cream van and those same two old ladies are fussing over her as if she's come back from death's door and I am so ashamed that combined with the heat, I think I'm going to explode. I think they say something to her about how wonderful it must be to have a lovely big sister to look after you and I feel resentful and my little sister looks rebellious - like I want to be saddled with her and like she'll ever do anything I say - and eventually we drag ourselves away and round the corner to where the ice-cream van is parked, serving the few children of the village.

They all stared at us, unblinking, like children do with other children they haven't sized up yet, and let us through to get our ice-creams.

'Sauce with that?' asked the ice-cream man. We didn't have enough money. The other children, with flakes or strawberry sauce, or lollies, looked at us, still unblinking - no indication of emotion, either pity or smugness. Still sizing us up.

Two little girls going back up the hill.

'I wish I had strawberry sauce' little sister said sadly. She didn't try the puppy dog thing on me, she knew it wouldn't work. But I felt sorry for her, clambering up the slope in this scorching heat on her little legs.

I looked up to the mysterious fforest for inspiration and said 'guess what, I can do magic.'

'Can you? Honest to God?'

'Yes. Come on, stand still.' I waved my hands over her melting ice-cream and intoned: 'By magic skill and magic force, I pour an invisible strawberry sauce.'

'Honest to God? Cross you heart and hope to die?' she said.

'Honest to God. Cross my heart and hope to die.' I replied firmly. She took a lick and smiled. She put her free (very) sticky hand in mine and we carried on up the hill.

'I never knew you could do magic' she said.

Well, she was a pain and an embarrassment, but she was my little sister. And right now we only had each other. But looking back, I do wonder if she did the howling on purpose before the sermon started.

HARBOUR MOUTH

As usual, dinner choked her and she ate barely anything. Sam didn't notice but poured her more wine. She drank some white. Then some red. As usual, she went to bed drained, pincers at her temples and took paracetamol and ibruprofen, and valerian because otherwise how would she sleep?

Sam was still watching TV. What was on TV tonight? Nothing.

She quietly packed a bag and wrote him a note. 4.40am every day and she was wide awake, her mind churning, churning, options like the doors off one of those unending corridors. Is the answer here? Or here? What had been the question? When the alarm went off her body ached, her eyes leaden. One foot in front of the other, shower, wake the kids, make breakfast, put on the face, do the hair, say goodbye to Sam, take the kids to school, late again, tutting stay-at-home mums watching her as they gossip before going for coffee or to walk the dog or clean their clean houses. Go to work. Endless emails, like the fairytale with the self-filling purse only with the opposite effect. The fuller the inbox, the more drained she felt. Rushing to get the task done for the vague thanks she'd get, providing data so that someone else would get the praise. What did it all mean anyway? Who wanted those endless stats? What did I do in work today? Nothing.

Rushing to get back for school pick-up. Late again. Angry teacher talking to her as if she was six. Driving home with the kids, 'what did you do in school today?' 'Nothing - what's for tea?' At home, the overflowing laundry, the pointless cooking of tea - prodding of broccoli, shovelling of pasta.

She tried to put all this in the note, waiting for the valerian to kick in and took more painkillers.Who would even miss her really? Exemplary employee, caring wife and mother - just functions. They'd miss the functions. How could they miss her? She had been lost a long long time. She tried to write this down, but it was hard to put it into words. She wasn't sure what she was writing.

The next day at 4.40am, she slipped out of bed and out of the house. She got to the coast and wondered vaguely if she'd shut the front door. She imagined the house - wide open, wondering where she'd gone - the overflowing laundry, the untidy rooms, the toys crying 'organise us!' and the fresh air blowing in whispering 'she's gone, she's gone' and the children and Sam sleeping on and on until they woke and tried to remember what she looked like and life going on without her.

She got to the coast and looked at the harbour bridge shiny in the dawn.

She didn't remember it being so long, the end was barely visible, the other side of the harbour mouth hazy and clean. Weren't there buildings there? Where was the traffic? Maybe it was always this quiet at 4.40am. Was it still 4.40am? No it must be later, time for the alarm to go off. Surprising there is no traffic.

She starts to walk across the bridge. Why am I walking? Didn't I bring the car? Never mind. It's peaceful here but looks even more peaceful there. The buzzing, the humming, the relentless noise of her mind is silent. Nothing can be heard, not the sea, nor the wind, nor the town behind her. Is the town behind her? She doesn't want to turn and look - the other side of the bridge is more inviting.

There is a person coming towards her, as vague as the bridge. It is calling to her. It must be shouting because it's so far away she can't tell if it's male or female, but the voice is like a whisper, she closes her eyes to hear better.

'Not yet,' it says, 'Go back, go back, here is some strength, go back, go back' and rain starts to fall on her from the clear blue sky.

'Come back come back,' and she opens her eyes and Sam is holding her, his tears falling on her face, and she is in her bed and he is holding her and he has her letter in his hand, crushed against her, 'you didn't wake when the alarm went off, I didn't know, I didn't know' and he pulls her up to himself, crying into her hair and he has her letter in his hand, crushed against her with its scrawled words: 'I'm lost. I'm so tired. I want to sleep forever. Find me.'

INSIDE

The sudden downpour took them by surprise as they lolled on the grass outside the cathedral. 'Quick, inside' said Izzy, grabbing Em's arm. She avoided the neat pensioners trying to encourage a donation and sat them down close to the door so they could get out as soon as possible.

You couldn't hear the rain. In fact you could hear very little, just the tourists wandering about taking photos, passing on the stone floor: click click click tap tap tap.

A long way down towards the other end people were just sitting.

'How boring,' said Izzy, leaning awkwardly to get a selfie of herself with the vaulted ceiling looming above her.

Em suddenly felt tired. Not from the holiday or late nights, but just tired. It was like being in a car that had been rushing along and suddenly stopped so that all the things in the back crashed into you. All the things in the back of Em's mind were crashing into her.

She thought about how she'd started to write a postcard to Grandma and was just about to sign her name when she remembered Grandma had died. She saw her future opening up in front of her: no longer at college, no longer supported by her parents, just her – responsible. She wondered if she would be loved, if life would make sense, if she would be worthwhile.

Em felt panic rising and tuned Izzy out, staring towards the brilliant stained glass window, sparkling even with a rain storm outside; and she looked at the people just sitting. Were they communing? Or just being still?

Tears filled Em's eyes, as she sat there feeling lost. Was this praying? She wasn't religious. She didn't have any words to say, so could it be praying - just laying your hurt and worry out?

She felt a hum in the air, like someone saying 'don't be afraid, be at peace,' and in her mind's eye, saw herself enveloped in comforting arms. And the things which been crashing into her, fell and dissolved.

THE GOOD WIFE

Charlotte stood obediently behind her husband, loathing him. The splendour of the foyer rose majestically around her, from gleaming marble floors, through a forest of bright pillars to ceilings garlanded with swooping loops of flowers and gilded leaves. To the side, an enormous staircase led, one hoped, to rooms of sufficient comfort to allow for sleep regardless of the noise of the city beyond the windows. But right now, Charlotte would have slept on the marble floor itself, she was so exhausted.

This was the first time Edmund had brought them to his regular hotel and the journey up from the country had been unpleasant and tiresome, even the first class carriage uncomfortably busy, and Edmund had refused to let her travel in the ladies' only carriage with Mary and the children. Instead she had found herself suffocating in a cloud of crinolines with the other first class ladies, wreathed in the cigar smoke of their escorts. Now Charlotte felt filthy and drained. She looked round at Mary and the children. They looked as she felt, little Amelie swaying on her feet. Mary appeared more depressed than usual, the grey round her eyes enhanced by travelling. Charlotte bit her lip as the girl caught her glance then looked away. She was going to have to do something soon. She had noticed how much more absent Edmund was and how much he frequented the nursery and saw in Mary's face the revulsion she herself had felt when trying to avoid his painful fondles and pinches after she had reluctantly agreed to his proposal. Her resistance then had inflamed him but now that she was a wife, and she had no choice but to be compliant, his ardour had dulled to a perfunctory exercise with no affection and little passion. The only pinches she now received were, along with the gripping of her arms, his reaction to any time she tried to disagree with him. Too late, she now realised why they were never able to keep young maids in their employ for very long.

'Edmund, might Mary and the children sit down? Amelia is so tired.' Charlotte pleaded.

Edmund turned and glared, 'One would have thought they'd had enough sitting down, but very well. I really don't understand this delay.'

They were in line waiting to be seen by the receptionist, who was being harangued by an irritated gentleman. A small rough crowd had followed them in on their arrival, managing to get past the doorman and pushing and shoving around them, too numerous for the hotel staff to evict easily. A boot boy had been despatched for a constable to assist. Charlotte drew her cloak and handbag close and tried to make herself small. She looked round at the children, leaning on Mary's shoulders and wished that Edmund might consider his wife needed protection. Edmund was ignoring her as usual however and simply complaining quietly and irritably about having to wait. The push behind them became greater. Small boys were slyly making attempts on pockets while others distracted.

Edmund turned and one of the young men leaned in and hissed very low and steadily: 'We've been following you ever since I recognised you at the station. You bastard. I remember what you did to my girl and now I've come for you.'

Was there a flicker in Edmund's face? It was all so fast, Charlotte never knew. The young man lunged forward and Edmund staggered slightly then righted himself, looking furious. The young man started to run and the crowd of ruffians surrounded him, hiding him in their midst as they pushed through the doors.

Everyone stared after them for a while, wondering what had happened and seconds passed before Charlotte turned and saw the hilt of a knife coming out of Edmund's back.

'Edmund! You've been stabbed!' she exclaimed, 'Quickly, come and sit down!'

The man immediately in front of them turned and went pale, making sympathetic noises but increasing his distance.

'Get it out!' demanded Edmund.

'No - that's not the right thing to do, I'm sure of it,' contradicted Charlotte, trying to steer him towards a seat. He was looking pale but otherwise seemed in control and angry. She called out: 'Please! Someone fetch a doctor, my husband is stabbed.'

'Get it out!' Edmund repeated.

'No!' she argued, 'I'm sure it's not the right thing to do. I'm sure father told me..'

'Oh you and your precious father,' snapped Edmund, 'spoiling you, thinking you could understand things. As if his daughter could follow him into medicine. Do as you are bid.'

'Edmund, truly…'

'I command you. Obey me!'

He had slumped now and was half lying on the floor, partially supported by her arm. He was very grey.

'Better do as your husband tells you, my dear' said the man in front of them, 'he's sure to know best.'

With what strength he had, Edmund wrenched her hand and tried to guide it to his back until it was touching the shaft.

Edmund furious, spoke slowly but with clenched teeth, 'Do…as….you…are….bid. Take…. it… out.'

In desperation, she looked into his face, the man she had feared from the moment he asked for her hand when she had so little option but to accept, then round to Mary and the children. Mary, almost as white as Edmund, trying to shield her little daughter and her young son, the boy Edmund bullied and beat until he wet the bed and cried in the night. Closing her eyes, Charlotte pulled the dagger slowly and sat on the floor of the foyer, under the gilded garlands, watched by the dimming eyes of her husband, his blood slowly staining the silk of her dress.

ALFIE

Alfie thought she was a witch, the woman that lived next door to their new home, but the other boys said no, she was just a mad old biddy, good for sweets at Halloween if you threatened her good and proper.

Alfie's mum didn't like those boys. She said they were nasty pieces of work and manipulating him. Alfie didn't know what manipulating meant but Mum didn't understand. He was the new kid and he was a bit of a brain. No-one really bothered to try and make friends. They all had their groups already - he was just an outsider. But these two took him under their wing straight away. He didn't exactly like them, but he wasn't sure what would happen if he didn't go along with them.

Alfie's mum said she was worried about him, she thought he'd get into trouble at school. But Jonesie and Baz said she just didn't understand a good time, a bit of a laugh.

'Tell you what,' said Jonesie, when they got bored of chucking things in the river, 'let's go and check out your neighbour's house. I could just see round her at Hallowe'en and she had some right old junk inside. I bet she's got something worth checking out. Come on Angel-face - you can charm her.'

'Wish you'd stop calling me Angel-face' complained Alfie.

Baz just cuffed him, 'your face is our fortune' he said, 'but we could soon change it.'

Alfie felt uncomfortable about the whole thing. He wished he was back at his old school with his old friends. He didn't really want to bother Mrs Smith, not just because he was slightly scared of her, but because it didn't feel right. Maybe he shouldn't have worried. Mrs Smith seemed quite happy to see them, even though Baz had dumped some toads he'd dug out of hibernation just inside her door on Hallowe'en. Perhaps she really was just a mad old biddy.

'Hello lads,' she said, smiling, 'I've just made some cake - would you like some?'

'Not half,' said Jonesie and Baz together. Alfie hung back and couldn't meet Mrs Smith's eyes. He didn't know what the others had planned, but he knew it wouldn't be right. But Mrs Smith unexpectedly lifted his chin and made him look at her. 'Trust your instincts and you won't go wrong' she whispered, 'Be brave, don't be afraid to be on your own. You are strong when you are true to yourself.' Alfie had no idea what she was on about, but he felt even worse. He could see, just over Mrs Smith's shoulder, Baz and Jonesie pocketing stuff from the overcrowded bungalow. He wasn't a thief. What would Mum say? He could imagine the disappointment in her face if she knew, after all she'd gone through too. The disappointment would be worse than any punishment. 'Mrs Smith...' he whispered, 'I'm sorry but they're...' He tried to point but she pulled his hand down and gave him a big wink.

'Come on lads!' she called out brightly, 'I'll get you some cake and then you can be off to play, like good boys!'

She wandered off into the kitchen, shuffling in her slippers and Baz and Jonesie rolled eyes at each other. Play?? Like they were four or something?

It seemed like seconds later that they were outside with three portions of cake. She'd wrapped Alfie's in girly paper and the other two sniggered.

'Here,' said Baz 'Let's go round to yours and we can show you our stash.'

In Alfie's room, Baz and Jonesie unwrapped their cake, refusing to share Alfie's piece on the grounds it was wrapped in pink paper and pulled things out of their pockets. They were toys. Really old fashioned toys. Alfie stared in fascination at them - their colours were sober and dull but they were beautiful - you could sense that immense care had gone into painting them. They were slightly worn around the edges, as if once upon a very long time ago, a child had played with them for hours on end.

One of the toys was a Jack-in-a-Box. The box was painted in red and gold, with little blue dots and white stars. The winding handle had been bright, but most of the paint had worn off and it was dull iron coloured. The other toy was a smart but baffled looking boy in a funny green and gold uniform with a sort of cap on his head, pushing a brown suitcase. A silver key came out of the side of the suitcase. They were beautiful.

'Let's smash em!' said Baz.

'No!' said Jonesie, 'Not yet - they might be worth something.'

'You reckon?' Baz was incredulous.

'Wonder what happens if you wind them up?' wondered Jonesie.

Baz wound the key on the suitcase and it ran along the floor. The boy did somersaults over the top of the case and ran behind, then somersaults and ran behind. It did this for a while and then stopped. The Jack-in-the-Box took a few turns on the handle and the lid opened. A slightly baffled looking clown jumped out and waved about for a while on his spring. Then the toys were still and the boys looked at them.

'Let's smash em!' said Baz.

'Yeah - let's smash em!' said Jonesie.

'No!' shouted Alfie.

'What's your problem, Angel-face?' sneered Baz, 'Scared of Mrs dopey Smith?'

'No… We've got cake to eat - give us some energy, then I'll er…' Alfie wasn't sure what he was going to do. But the boys shrugged and unwrapped their cake, munching on it and eyeing the ancient toys as if to wonder how best to destroy them.

Alfie was never sure what happened next exactly. As he ate the cake, the room went swimmy and Baz and Jonesie went out of focus. There were a few moments when everything seemed to go dark and then he came to and was staring at Baz and Jonesie and they were staring at the toys and smirking. Alfie couldn't bear it.

'Don't smash them!' he shouted, 'just leave them alone. They're…'

Baz and Jonesie exchanged glances. Come to think of it, they didn't look quite the same, or did they? Alfie's eyesight still didn't seem to be working. Baz now looked slightly baffled and Jonesie looked smarter than usual. And they looked kinder. Sort of cheeky but not nasty.

'Nah - we're not going to smash them.' said Jonesie, 'They're really …. I'm not sure of the word,

I've … we've got some catching up to do. What's your name again?'

'Alfie.'

'Nice to meet you Alfie. Er… can you tell us where we live? And er…. what our names are?'

Alfie showed them out and pointed to their houses. They waved at him and looking slightly lost but quite happy, made their way home.

Alfie went back into his room, picked up the toys and looked at them. The boy with the suitcase looked bad tempered all of a sudden. Alfie turned the handle on the Jack-in-a-Box and the clown that popped out looked angry and also…. looked like Baz??

Alfie shook his head, he just wanted things to go back to how they were. He knew he was too old, but he really felt like a cuddle with Mum. He picked up the toys and took them back to Mrs Smith.

'I'm sorry,' he said, 'I tried to tell you they'd taken them. '

'It's all right son,' she said, 'It's hard being a loner sometimes isn't it?'

'I'll think about what you said,' he added, 'I'll try and not let them get me into trouble.'

'They won't' she said firmly, 'I've seen to that.' She grinned at him.

Alfie stopped looking at his feet and looked up at Mrs Smith and then he looked at the toys. The more he looked at them, the more he thought they looked like Baz and Jonesie.

'It's them isn't it?' he gasped.

Mrs Smith nodded. 'Yup.' she said, 'there comes a point when bad lads need a lesson.'

'So those other kids... Er when will you turn Baz and Jonesie back?'

Mrs Smith grinned 'Oh, about a hundred years should sort them out' she told him, 'that's how long it took to improve the other two...'

PASSING THROUGH

Once she had been a girl, young and innocent, looking into a bright future. Now she was a woman, wishing she could unsee the dark six years of her past.

Once she had been a girl hoping that one day she'd find a paradise, now she was a woman who had been released from hell.

She and her sister had been young and strong enough to be useful for a while. But when the rescuers came they were shells, bones held together with sinew, skin stretched paper thin. Once she had been proud and pretty, curling her hair and dreaming up new dresses. But when the rescuers came she no longer cared that she was half naked and her lovely hair shaved, lice crawling frantically to find sustenance.

Her sister held her hand tightly as they left for the refugee camp. They didn't look back, even though Mother was there, gassed on arrival, her limbs forever tangled with those of friends and strangers in one of a thousand unmarked pits. But in the refugee camp, so nearly safe, cholera took her sister and she was left on her own.

Her body healed. In the end, if they are not destroyed, that's what bodies do. But her heart drowned in unspent tears.

Eventually, it was time to leave. She tidied her donated dress, tucked her short hair under the donated hat, picked up her donated coat and her donated clothes and made her way home. She knew she was going only to say goodbye.

There was no-one left. Or at least, none of her family. She was the only one. Some of the old neighbours came and greeted her and wept. Some of them avoided her eyes and sidled away. The place was sick with shame and absence. Her old home was occupied by strangers and there was nothing to do but leave for a new life.

At the station, she shuddered. The day was cold but bright and there were only trains not cattle trucks, but all those shoving fearful ghosts surrounded her. Still, she just had to be brave just one more time.

She raised her head and straightened her back, looking along the platform.

A thin young man was sitting on a case, looking at photographs. He was shivering. She knew the wind penetrated his gauntness and knew that under his hat, his hair was too short, grown back from being shorn. She watched him shiver again and wondered if it was cold or emotion as he turned over the pictures and swallowed as if to stop himself from crying. Maybe it wasn't just his family on those photographs, maybe hers were there too.

She didn't hesitate for long and walked up to him.

She only stood over him for a second before saying: 'you look cold, do you want to borrow my coat to go over your shoulders till the train comes in?'

The young man looked up and blinked. For a moment they were both silent, startled, seeing past the scars and starvation to soft remembered faces and then shyly they smiled at each other.

'Hello Avigail' said David.

And she put her case down, placed her hand in his and sheltering under the coat together, they turned their eyes down the track which led to hope.

THE LAST CHALLENGE

Edward stopped, exhausted. His pack weighed heavy, full as it was with treasures collected en route. He was the only survivor and beyond him was the final challenge. All he had to do was get to the mountain across the lake, enter a cave, kill a dragon and find the last piece of the quest, then he could return triumphant and claim the Princess and half her father's kingdom. There were plenty of boats to choose from and all of them sturdy, but he needed to collect himself first. He looked around and saw a tavern. It stood on the shore and looked out across the lake towards the mountains and it was welcoming. Someone stood outside beckoning him over. Edward smiled and hoisting his pack again, strode across.

There was warm beer and hot bread and spiced sausages, dripping fat. Edward sat back in his chair and considered the last stage of his journey. It was a beautiful place: serene, relaxing, quiet. He sighed and started to rise from his chair.

'More beer sir?' said the waiter, looming silently, 'or do you have to be gone?'

Edward opened his mouth and paused. Did he have to be gone? Did he really? Do I have a choice? he asked himself.

'There's always a choice,' said the waiter, as if he could read minds. 'It's nice here, steady trade in summer; time to think in winter; plenty of game and beer; warm, funny, kind, cuddly women. Never be rich in money, but there are different kinds of wealth perhaps.'

Edward sat back and thought about the Princess. She was very beautiful but her eyes flashed when she did not get her way. He thought about the half a kingdom. Why was her father so keen to hand it over? Warring nobility? Rebellious peasantry? Scheming merchants? He thought for a long time.

'Any jobs going?' he asked eventually 'I have a few bits I could give you to pay my rent till I proved myself.'

The waiter smiled: 'the more the merrier,' he said and went to get more beer.

FIFTEEN

The homework assignment is gathering dust and is still totally pointless.

Mum is nagging again: 'when your great grandmothers were fifteen, they weren't out all the time messing about with their friends. They just wished they could continue their education. When your grandmothers were fifteen, they were only a year away from college. They didn't sit around waiting for things to happen - they made things happen, well, they would have if they hadn't got married first.'

'So what were you doing back when you were fifteen?' I retort, 'fighting off dinosaurs with your crinoline?'

Mum's eyes glaze over slightly, her memory receding into memories of kids with mohicans and safety pins through their noses.

'I was mostly waiting for this boy to realise I was the one he wanted. And drawing pictures of lonely girls staring into rivers. And writing stories about not being understood.'

'So you were waiting for things to happen and desperate to get married then?'

'I didn't want to marry him!' she falters 'just go out with him. Anyway, the point is..'

'The point is, if I do this assignment, I won't waste my life. It will totally change my whole future if I do this assignment. I will be successful and have a great career and never look back. If I don't do this assignment, my life will be ruined and I'll end up a bored housewife with a crap job wishing for the rest of my life I'd done this assignment. My whole life depends on this assignment. When I'm as old as you, I will look back and say "that assignment I had when I was 15, that was what changed my world." That's what you're saying.'

Mum rolls her eyes and sighs.

'The point is..' she struggles on.

'Mum!' I interrupt again, 'Tell me one, just one, assignment you had when you were fifteen. Apart from maths. Tell me the one piece that put you were you are now.'

She goes glazed again, there is a very long pause. 'You had to draw the table under the bunsen burner or Mr Henderson knocked marks off. And Mr Skipton said my picture of Lake Erie looked like an amoeba. And I wrote a short story once that was brilliant but I never got it back. I always thought Mr Williams pinched it.'

'And that's it? So go on - what was the point of all that?'

Another long pause. 'Goodness knows. To be fair, my Lake Erie drawing probably did look like an amoeba.' She sits down and gives me a hug, 'anyway, what's this assignment then?'

I push the interesting stuff aside and show her the title: 'Homework: arguments for and against.'

'I've got to be honest,' says Mum, 'that's a pretty crap assignment.'

'Did you get the boy in the end?' I ask.

'Yeah, eventually, but not till I was sixteen,' she says, 'we used to do our homework together sometimes.' She pauses and grins. 'Well in theory anyway.'

Parents are gross.

KINDLING

The thing was, one full-moon night, the husband snoring and the insomnia and the restless legs just got too much and I thought 'why not go for a walk in the woods - you're awake anyway' so I did.

I wasn't completely stupid. I took a roll mat and a sleeping bag so if I did get overcome with fatigue I wouldn't freeze to death and I took my e-reader for something to do when I was still awake. The moon was luminous but not bright enough to read by.

Was I afraid of what I'd meet? Not really, who goes out at night nowadays? They're all indoors online or watching TV. Burglars? - what's to steal in a wood? Murderers? - Nah. Doggers? - too muddy - couldn't get a car in. Ghosts? - don't be ridiculous.

It was a pleasant walk. The air was autumnal, drifts of mist trailed around me from time to time, the moon fractured through the branches and my feet crunched satisfactorily on the first fallen leaves.

Eventually I found the big oak in the middle of a small clearing renowned in earlier months for its bluebell carpet. I settled down under the tree inside the sleeping bag and got the e-reader out. I was about to turn it on when I became aware of moths fluttering round me, hovering over the screen. It was a bit irritating but to be expected. I was about to wave them away when one of them spoke.

'What's it doing?' it said.

I looked up and realised that it wasn't moths surrounding me, it was ethereal semi-transparent people, the 'moths' were sparkling bits of their clothes catching the moonbeams.

'Look,' said one of the people, 'it's got its mouth open. Do you think we've startled it?'

Well yes they had. I managed to ask them who they were. Really I wanted to know WHAT they were, but that seemed a little impolite and there were more of them than me. Transparent or otherwise, they were tall and fit looking and were regarding me as if I were some sort of insect they'd rarely seen.

'We're the fair folk,' said one of them, an ebony beauty with braids.

'And you're trespassing,' said one of her companions, a cold eyed blond Adonis.

'Er, I'm sorry,' I said politely, 'I didn't realise the wood belonged to anyone in particular.'

'It does at full-moon in September,' he informed me 'and now you must pay forfeit.'

'Do you think we should swap its children for changelings?' said a red head female.

'Don't bother,' I replied, 'They're both teenagers - I think you've already done it.'

They stared down at me in eerie silence for some time and after a while, I thought 'this is all in my head - ignore them and they'll go away' and turned my e-reader back on.

There was an intake of breath. The fair folk leaned forward. 'What is that?' the male asked.

There was something like awe in their previously supercilious faces. 'It's a....' I thought for a moment, 'it's a library of books - look it has one hundred at least inside but it weighs no more than a... than a few gold coins.' I showed them the library and opened up a few books. I managed, despite their intense stares, to find 'Midsummer Night's Dream' and quote a bit of Titania. There was a combined intake of breath.

'That's deep magic,' said the braided female, 'where did a mortal come by such a thing?'

'My mother gave it to me,' I told them quite truthfully.

They conferred for a while. I heard one of them whisper 'her mother must be a great witch' which is a harsh thing to say about my sweet old mum. Eventually they pulled apart and the male addressed me.

'We will let you go,' he pronounced, 'provided you leave behind your magic library and never return to this place at midnight ever again.'

Well, to be honest, I don't believe in this sort of stuff at all, but they were really giving me the creeps. So I got up, clambered inelegantly out of the sleeping bag and walked carefully backwards to the edge of the clearing. They followed me silently with steely glares and started to reach out their hands; hands which didn't look as beautiful as their faces. At the edge of the clearing, I gently laid the e-reader down and as they bent to retrieve it I ran like blazes.

*****

So now I've got to get a new e-reader before my beloved spots that it's gone and asks what's happened to it. Only thing is I'll just have to buy one. I somehow don't think the insurance company will believe that the old one is away with the fairies.

SURPLUS ENERGY

A stranger approached me at lunchtime. She told me she was from the future and needed my help.

I nearly choked on my burger, but thought, best humour her, she looks like she could outrun me.

'What sort of help?' I asked, sipping my cola.

'I need your security pass to get into your office so I can get to the top of the building, because it's the tallest one in the town.'

'They're pretty strict on checking people.' I told her.

'It'll be fine, just escort me in and get me a visitor pass.'

'What's in it for me?' I queried.

'What else have you got planned? I represent a world of possibilities.' She coaxed, 'Trust me, if I get this sorted out, things will be so different for you. I promise, your self confidence will increase, your prospects, everything. And I'll always use you for liaison.'

I'm not sure why I believed her, but my life was dull, I was unimportant and there was something mesmerising about her. I figured that although I was right down the bottom of the heap in my organisation, the few years I'd had in admin had been mostly spent blagging: 'the cheque's in the post', 'we'll get back to you tomorrow,' 'yes I totally sympathise'. So 'this lady is here for a meeting, please can she have a visitor's pass?' shouldn't be too much of a problem.

It wasn't and without any trouble, I got her to the top of the building. Our town's really small so the roof was only twenty floors up and I could see for miles: my toylike town, the fields, the villages. It felt like the whole world spread out below and for a few moments I had the dizzying feeling that I was in control of it.

The stranger got this something out of her back pack and attached it to the lightning conductor, pressing buttons until it started pulsating. Then she turned to me and grinned.

'Just wait: in a moment, you'll feel like a new man.'

I didn't know whether to feel worried or excited. She smiled brightly at me and stepped forward, 'I suppose I ought to explain. I'm from the future. People like me will be fixing these things on roofs all over the world over the next few hours.'

'Why?'

'Thing is, we've run out of fossil fuels, want to avoid nuclear, but still need energy. What is a source of energy? Fat. We're all thin. But after a while we worked how to utilise, sorry, liaise with a previous generation. You. When this device kicks in, it will suck out the excess fat from every overweight person in a three hundred mile radius and transport ninety percent through time to our world. The other ten percent will be transferred to the starving in your developing nations so that they have energy to compete with your developed nations. Give it five mins and you'll be much much thinner.'

Then she disappeared.

It took ten minutes for me to lose three stone. First I'm on the top of my office building watching a stranger attach something to the lightning conductor, next thing she's disappeared, I'm looking in my cola wondering what was in it and heading for the lift. By the time I get to the ground floor, I'm having to hold my trousers up to stop them falling off.

Walking back into the office, smug people coming back from their gym sessions found the undisciplined doughnut munchers such as me also comparing sudden transformations.

All over the world, my little town included, obesity ceased within two hours. There was a bit of a lull while everyone adjusted. Ten percent of the excess human fat was transmitted to the starving in our current world. Ninety percent of the excess human fat was transmitted to the future to replace fossil and nuclear fuels for our descendants. What could go wrong?

Well for a start, the bottom fell out of the diet and exercise industries. Then manufacturers increased the cost of clothes, even though less fabric was involved. Obesity clinics closed but eating disorder clinics mushroomed. No amount of under-eating made a difference to those who looked in the mirror and saw not perfection but fat, they just got their portion of the ten percent destined for the starving.

Everyone else pretty much just ate every high calorie food they could and stayed slim. Yet…without the masochistic, guilty shame of feeling the grease or sugar on your chin, it was not the same. Art galleries found that Botticelli and Rubens were back into fashion as people looked longingly at rounded stomachs and pillowy breasts.

Meanwhile robot development increased exponentially to enable people to enjoy more leisure time with their newly perfect bodies. Factories, shops, offices, farms, all workers up to senior management were slowly replaced by machines. So what's wrong with lots of leisure time? People got bored, that's what. And a bored well fed human is one of the most dangerous animals there is.

Then there was a sugar and lard shortage. All foods shot up in price.

And then even healthy food ran out.

Internationally, everyone's weight dropped below healthy levels and the machines stopped transmitting. Twenty years after their first appearance, the future people returned. The woman whom I'd taken to the lightning conductor sought me out and tutted.

'We didn't think you'd manage it so soon,' she said as if it had all been my fault there was mass famine and all the fields were dustbowls.

'Can't you send the fat back to us?' I asked

She snorted. 'Your inability to keep us in fuel is causing our systems to fail. We need power more than you need fat.'

I got angry: 'people are starving. The whole world: starving.'

'You've had your chance,' she said coldly, 'whereas we're your descendants and need the fuel.'

She suddenly went out of focus, said 'well I suppose that's the only thing to do', refocussed and turned on a smile which reached only as far as her cheek bones.

'We'll help,' she murmured in a different tone, 'we're going to show you how to feed yourselves and how to replenish the land.'

'Will we be fat enough to send you the energy you want?'

She snorted and then remembered she was trying to be nice.

'Hardly,' she said, 'but we'll have a mutually beneficial solution to our energy problem and your overpopulation problem. I just need you to get people in this town rounded up, er, gathered together.

It took a while, but I did it.

All over the world, people from the future explained how to grow insects and highly nutritious vegetables. If you ever thought you'd had difficulty feeding broccoli to a toddler, you should try feeding seaweed and locusts to a forty year old.

That was phase one.

Then came phase two. Tackling the excess population. All over the world, redundant people, replaced by robots, were given the chance to be transported to the future and work there.

I tell you that was the easiest thing I've done. Rounding people up, sorry gathering people up for a future in the future. It must have been good. They never came back to visit.

Five years passed and I became one of those replaced by a robot. Can you imagine how that feels? 'Good luck on the personal development plans,' I said to the robot team leader, patting it on what I like to think of its head as I left, carrying my leaving card with its two human signatures and twenty sets of zeros and ones.

There was nothing left for me but to join the queue of people transported to the future.

We arrived inside some massive building, gleaming and humming but without windows. The woman signing us in was surprised to see me. 'Oh it's you,' she said. I had the feeling she was worried about who she'd use as a go-between from now on.

'It's me,' I said, 'can you tell me what my job will be?'

She looked at me with something akin to pity.

'Didn't you understand?' she said as gently as she could, 'We need to create power. We haven't got fossil fuel, we don't like nuclear, we can't access your fat anymore, we just need people to run turbines.'

'I don't know how engines work,' I told her with some concern, 'I'm a paper-pusher.'

'There is no engine,' she said almost kindly, 'it's a treadmill. All the excess people from your era - like you -what good does it do to starve slowly to death in your own time over many years unwanted and despised? Here in your future - you'll be appreciated and we'll make sure your death is quick and painless.'

She patted me gently on the shoulder, 'But the key thing to remember is that for the short time you're with us: you can eat anything you want.'

THE LETTERS

She had to find them. It was so dark and she couldn't find her way. Where was her room? Where was it? How could she not find her own room? All she cared about was in that room, her chap box with her little bit of savings, her two dresses, her pretty ribbons, the little bit of fichu her mother had made her before she left home, the tears woven into the lace itself.

And the letters. His precious letters. Every night she touched them and smelt them and unfolded them. If there was a little stub of candle to light or it was summer, she looked at them too. Tracing his name with her work-sore fingers. She could not read them, but she could remember each word, each word he'd read out to her before he went away. She only had to keep reading them and he would come back to her. She could not leave those things. They were her whole life.

It was getting warmer now. People were calling to her. Or perhaps they had stopped calling to her and the shouts she heard were just shouts, screams even. Her eyes were watering and her throat tightening. She could no longer draw breath. She could see the gleam of flames from under the floor boards and hear them devouring their way up the stairs, up through the main room, up to the bedrooms, up to her in the attic.

She could just make out a window and crawled to it; no longer sure whose window it was. But it was hers, and under the bed, her box. She felt inside it and pulled out the bundle of letters, warm now as if his love was in them. She tried to sigh but it was a cough. She realised she could no longer breathe.

She pressed her face against the tiny bit of glass. It was a poor window, a servant's window but she could see the whole town ablaze beyond it. And below, below she could just make out the landlord and his wife looking up at her, frantically beckoning to her. But there was no way down. She could hear the fire cackling on the landing and the smoke filled her lungs and she fell. Clasping the letters to her breast, she fell and was still.

THE CONTEST

As you know, we had been honing our psychic skills for generations yet we didn't see *Them* coming.

In the same way that we had learned how to project into each other's mind the image of ourselves that we choose, *They* had gone further and learned how to do the same with objects. Thus *They* had effectively camouflaged themselves, hidden in plain sight.

Let me explain. You look at me and see me as I wish you to. Thus you might perceive me as young or old and fat or thin and black or white etcetera depending entirely on what image I wish you to see. There is a me-ness which enables you to recognise me, but otherwise the layout of my face and body can be changed like clothes. You will be able to do this too, once you are adult.

Similarly, when *They* came, we saw our own drones and shuttles coming down out of the atmosphere, when in fact they were *Theirs* and *They* were huge and numerous.

What made the invasion the success it was however, was not simply *Their* cunning and numbers. It was the leeches.

Well that's what we called them. I am not sure now what they are exactly, whether organic or robotic. Sometimes I wonder if they even existed, whether they were some kind of projection which worked on our psyches instead. Whatever they were, and you, being so young, will not remember this, they were the means of our destruction.

You would see a cloud of them suddenly descend on maybe three or four people at once. It usually only took about ten of the leeches - their mouths had rows of needle sharp teeth and they latched on through clothes and shoes and drew blood none the less. Within seconds, before anyone could try and help, the person was drained and lifeless. The leeches, full of blood, then reproduced by division. Ten became twenty and sought two victims instead of one, then twenty became forty and so on. There was no escape. Every city, every town became a charnel house. And then the leeches were gone and *They* were in control.

Why some of us survived I don't know. Perhaps we weren't drained enough. Perhaps it was a decision on *Their* part. I can't even recall how we found each other, scattered as we were across the globe. I have a dim recollection of a never ending road, of thirst and hunger and emptiness, occasionally meeting another survivor and joining up, but never finding the ones we were looking for. You were a tiny infant I found next to a woman's body. No-one needed another mouth to feed but I picked you up anyway. I suspect *They* may have helped us, it is all very hazy. Perhaps *They* herded us like cattle before settling us all on this island and trying to work out what to do next.

We did attempt, in the early days, to show each other what we really looked like, but we were too exhausted and depressed to care.

And then one of *Their* leaders came. *It* asked us why *They* shouldn't simply wipe us out, the way *They* were systematically wiping out our towns and cities one by one. Clearing the land.

One person told *It* 'just put us out of our misery'. Another said what did *It* mean, *They* were destroying our cities. What about our culture, our history, our libraries? Notice: no-one cared too much about the financial institutions and bureaucracies.

It seemed puzzled. Why would we care? But *It* said that we needed to justify our existence and maybe *They* would negotiate about some of the culture.

'When *We* came, you were in the middle of a hundred wars all over this tiny little sphere, and in each of those wars you were intent on destroying each others' culture, each others' history and supplanting it with another one. How can *We*, as outsiders, decide which to save? *We* need to clear the land for ourselves. Let *Me* show you what you look like to *Us* and you can show what you believe yourselves to be and then *We* can decide.'

We cleared a space and it became an arena. We had no time to prepare and had to hope that in our weakened state we could manage this kind of telepathy.

It started. In the middle of the arena appeared image after image of cities in the middle of bombardment, the mangled bodies in the dust; destroyed temples and mosques and temples; paper fluttering in the wind; hands clasped in death.

We shifted uneasily. Without question we were all sitting with our own former enemies, had all been guilty by reason of nationality for one or other of those images. But someone managed to concentrate and projected images of rescues, of peace envoys, of forgiveness, of demonstrations: 'Not in my name.'

Next *It* displayed images of pampered pets and spoiled children and gluttonous adults, people fighting to get goods they didn't need against pictures of neglected children; starving people scrubbing in the dirt; emaciated women fetching water.

There was a pause and then someone managed to project images of people helping others to improve their life, people putting aside their luxuries and comfort to take in a troubled child, people working together to set up new projects to benefit their community.

Next *It* simply displayed a range of books, hovering in the air, holy books, political books. They spun and as they spun, hazy in the background you could see flame and hear weeping.

A voice called out: 'You cannot blame the book! That is like blaming the knife for the stabbing! It is the human who takes the book and destroys its meaning or takes the book and *discovers* its meaning.'

And an image took over of people in quiet contemplation, in soup kitchens, in worship, taking in strangers, giving alms.

'You are a corrupt and violent species!' *It* bellowed, 'You can do good and you can do evil. You create chaos and then you put it right. Why not simply leave things alone in the first place? *We* have all but wiped you out and you hate *Us*. But really, *We* were only speeding up what you started. Show *Me* one thing, just one thing that sets you apart from those leeches *We* set on you?'

There was a long pause and then, image after image appeared from all around the arena. They overlapped and interlinked as each of us projected a memory: holding hands with our mother on the way to school; a kiss from a grandparent; a kiss with a lover; the birth of a longed for child; the gentle passing of a loved one ... hundreds of images falling over themselves in a confused display of love. As they faded others appeared: the hug of friends; the comfort of strangers; the sun rising; two people leaning against each other and sharing a smile.

And then someone picked you up, yes you. Then a different child was held up and then another and someone shouted out: 'We still have hope!'

And singing started up. I don't know what the song was. Probably only two people knew the words, but we just joined in one by one anyway and sang what seemed to make sense.

Then there was utter silence. And *It* went away.

And here we are. I don't know if *They* will leave us alone. I don't know if we will learn from the past and make a better future. Sadly I fear we won't. I don't know if there is anything left in the world of the good things we had created. All I know is that if all we have left and all we take forward is love and hope, maybe we have justified our existence.

CATCHING THE POST

ALIX

Alix decided if she was going to go to the postbox, she might as well put her running gear on and run there. Or at least pretend to. David asked her what she thought she as doing.

'Have you seen the fog?' he argued, 'It was hell driving home. What on earth makes you want to go out in it? You can't see your hand in front of your face. You'll fall off the pavement and get run over or someone will attack you or something.'

Alix hadn't noticed the fog. She'd been stuck indoors all day with the laptop and her thoughts, tackling bureaucracy and sorting out the old letters and diaries discovered when her mother went into the hospital. And then somehow she'd felt the desperate urge to try once more with Amy.

'I need to get out,' she said, 'if it's that bad, I'll just go to the post box and back. If I don't go now it won't catch the first post.'

David looked at the letter and scowled. 'I don't know why you're wasting your time. She won't come.'

Alix looked at her husband - the stubborn set to his jaw masking the hurt pride, a characteristic he had passed down to their daughter. She swallowed the words she wanted to say. They had been said over and over. Someone had to give in and she was tired of it being her.

She pretended to do some stretches and opened the door.

'Won't be long,' she said.

She had never seen fog like it. It pressed against the walls like a pillow, as if it was trying to smother the house.

Still, the post box was so near she could have run there blind-fold and she really needed to get out. Maybe she'd just post the letter and come back, maybe she'd post the letter and run round the block. Maybe she'd just post the letter and go to the shops, just to clear her head.

JENNY

'Where do you think you're going?' said Jenny's mother, 'have you seen the fog?'

'I don't care,' said Jenny, pulling on her hat and buttoning her jacket, 'I've got to post this letter - it's got to get to Bill before he sails.'

'They won't let him have that leave you know. Anyway, for all you know he's sailed already. Don't you....'

Jenny opened the door and slammed it behind her before Mother asked her if she didn't know there was a war on. Again.

Mother opened the door and continued regardless, 'look at it - it's thicker than porridge. It's uncanny that's what it is. That's what your gran would say and she had the second sight. You go out in this you'll get run over, mark my words. And I've got a nice Woolton pie in the oven and it'll go to waste.'

Jenny took a breath and dug into the fog, it felt like mining. 'If I get run over, Arthur can have my portion. In fact, he can have it anyway, I'm not hungry.'

She stormed off. It was true, she wasn't hungry. Even if Woolton pie wasn't the most revolting thing made worse by a mother who could ruin even the blandest foods, she was aching from missing Bill. And she didn't know why she needed to have this weekend with him, maybe just a night, maybe an hour, even in some dingy little boarding house near the docks, but she did.

Distantly she could still hear her mother still moaning: 'it's not proper chasing after a man, even when he's your husband. Especially when he's your husband. Only fools marry when there's a war on.' Her voice faded away.

Even in the blackout Jenny could have walked to the post box in her sleep but she felt disorientated in the sheer darkness of the fog. It felt as if she in some horrible game of blind man's bluff. She kept slipping off the pavement into the road. It wasn't far now.

CHARLOTTE

Charlotte waited until Father fell asleep and carefully let herself out. The post box was set into the wall five houses away. She left the door on the latch and pulled it to. If she hurried she'd just about have enough time to catch the post.

She was so ashamed it hurt. How stupid she had been, how miserable she was. A whole day of weeping silently. What if he wouldn't forgive her? What if he thought she wasn't worth it? What if he didn't understand the fear that she felt? What if he didn't come back for her and she was stuck with Father forever, desiccating into a mad old maid.

Charlotte kept her head down and her coat wrapped tight round her. She had forgotten her hat in her haste and felt vaguely wanton. She couldn't even see the hem of her skirt, let alone the tips of her shoes as she rushed along. She tried to take a deep breath and realised it was not just the corset which stopped her from filling her lungs. It was the fog, impenetrable and almost edible.

She looked up to see if she could make out the post box, which was right next to a street lamp, but it was hard to make out whether the dim glimmer she could see was the lamp or light from an upstairs window.

Yes - here it was. How strange, it was glowing slightly, the only item of colour in the swirling grey.

Two other people were nearing it. Charlotte tried to make herself small. They looked very strange. Making out the shapes, she could tell that one was clearly a woman, but her skirts were short like a girl's. On the other hand, she was wearing a hat and Charlotte self-consciously touched her damp uncovered hair. The other person - it was hard to tell, but it also seemed to be a woman, although it was hard to make out what she was wearing. Some sort of trousers and some sort of shapeless jacket. And she was also hatless, her longish hair pulled back into a sort of tail like a horse.

Charlotte slowed. She didn't know what to do.

ALIX

The post box was glowing. That was the first thing Alix noticed. The next thing she noticed was that two other women were approaching. One was in a ridiculous long dress, creeping along apparently poised to run at the first threat and the other was dressed up in a dowdy suit with a rabbit's foot pinned on as a brooch. She was even wearing a hat. Alix was conscious of her running gear and felt immensely un-feminine.

JENNY

Jenny could see the postbox gleaming redly which was very odd. Then she realised that two others were approaching. One was dressed forty years or so out of date and the other looked as if she was wearing tight pyjamas. Were they ghosts? Her mother's words echoed in her mind: 'it's uncanny, that's what it is.'

Well nothing was going to stop her posting the letter. Once she'd done that she'd run.

'It's got to catch the post,' she said urgently, her voice shaking, 'whoever you are - please don't stop me.'

ALIX

'Why would I stop you?' Alix protested, taken aback, 'Mine needs to catch the post too. Why are you frightened of me?'

'Because you're ghosts.'

'I'm not a ghost,' Alix said, 'I'm from round the corner,' as if that precluded the supernatural. 'I just need to send a letter to my daughter.' She looked round at Charlotte hovering at the edge of what little light there was. If anyone was a ghost it was this young woman in Edwardian clothes, timid, a little older than the one in the old fashioned tweed suit. Yet she seemed so very much alive with emotion.

CHARLOTTE

Charlotte took a breath. She really hadn't much time, if Father came after her, he'd stop the letter being posted and that would be the end. Gerald would never know she'd changed her mind, that she was brave enough to go away with him after all.

'I need to post mine. If I don't...' Charlotte's voice petered out but she darted forward anyway. How strange, the panel on the front of the post box kept blurring - but she had to take the risk. The letter in her gloved hand slipped into the slot and as she let go, the two other women disappeared and she was on her own in the familiar street just a few doors away from her house. The fog was receding slightly and she ran for home to creep in through the door and close it gently. Now it was just a matter of waiting.

JENNY

Jenny looked at Alix nervously. Charlotte had posted her letter and instantly dissolved into the fog which was now thicker than ever, sucking at their faces.

Tears filled Jenny's eyes. 'I've got to post it.' she said, 'I don't know why, but I just know I have to post it. Whoever you are, please don't stop it getting through.' She took a firm step forward and pushed her letter into the box. As she let go, the woman in the pyjamas disappeared and she could hear her brother's voice calling her. She started back up the hill wondering why she had been so unnerved by the fog. It wasn't so bad. Jenny turned to look at the post box, dull and barely visible in the blacked out street. All she had to do now was wait.

ALIX

Alix stood in the gloom alone. The fog was now so dense she could feel it in her lungs and ears and filling up her eyes. The postbox continued to glow. What was the point in posting the letter? Maybe David was right. Maybe it was a waste of time. It was certainly old fashioned. Who wrote letters nowadays? It might not even get to Amy for days. But somehow, somehow it made sense. The calls and texts and messages and emails had gone unanswered, maybe it would take a letter to get their daughter to come home.

It seemed as if the fog had formed a barrier in front of the box. Alix hesitated. What was she afraid of? Failure? Humiliation? Disappointment? What did any of those things matter really? With a sense of forcing her way through cobweb, she posted the letter to Amy and stood back, waiting to disappear.

Nothing happened. She shook her head, damp with the fog which suddenly didn't seem much worse than usual. She could just make out the orange streetlights blurring but otherwise visible, marking her way home.

She let herself into the hall. Her hair was curling from the damp air and she suddenly felt grief overwhelm her. Mum would soon be gone, was nearly gone, just a frail shell of patient endurance; a softly held hand and barely audible words. And Amy didn't know. Amy, who had stormed out after that row with her father all those months ago, wouldn't contact her, didn't know how little time was left to see her grand-mother alive. There were things you couldn't put in texts or leave on answer phones - you just needed to say them face to face.

Alix pulled herself together as much as she could and walked into the kitchen. David was sitting at the table with the bundles of letters and diaries.

'Did you know your great great grandmother eloped?' he said, passing her a picture of a shy girl in Edwardian clothes.

'Yes I knew that.' said Alix, 'It worked out in the end. A year or so later they came back home and made peace with her father.' She tried not to say this pointedly as she took the photograph, frowning as she looked at it, the timid stranger somehow familiar, 'and he left them the house when he died. I think it was just round the corner, near the....'

She stopped. David didn't notice, now flicking through an 1940 diary. He frowned and rummaged in the box until he found the one for 1941, and a tele-gram, yellowed with age.

'Did you know your mother never met her own father?' he asked, 'In fact, it looks as if your mother might easily not have existed at all. Listen to your grandmother's diary: "thank goodness my letter caught the post and they let Bill have that weekend leave before he sailed, who knows when I'll see him again." That was November 1940 and as far as I can tell she never did see him again. Look, here's your mum being born August 1941 and then see this tele-gram came a few weeks later to say his ship had been torpedoed.'

He was silent. Alix leaned over and picked up a dusty rabbit's foot brooch half hidden by old letters and turned it over in her hands.

David was still looking at the diary. His voice was quiet. 'Makes you think doesn't it? All those moments when one small thing made all the difference.' He paused. 'Did you post that letter?'

'Yes' said Alix, 'I nearly didn't but in the end it suddenly seemed the most important thing in the world.'

David took back the photo of Alix's great great grandmother and stared at it for a while. 'I think there's some dust in my eye,' he said, rubbing the corner and leaving the room. He didn't come back and after a while Alix went to look for him. The sitting room door was ajar and she was about to open it when she heard his voice low, tearful and insistent.

'Amy: don't hang up,' he was saying, 'don't hang up please. I'm sorry for what I said, please listen, come home, your mum needs you. I need you. I'm sorry - Amy, please just come home.'

INTERNAL MEMO

It has come to the attention of Management, that staff (particularly those of the longest service and more mature years) are complaining that 'we used to have more fun at work in the good old days'.

Management is also concerned that staff state that they feel unable to express their views in team meetings and that this may be contributing to higher than usual levels of stress in the workforce.

Management has also noted that despite annual health-awareness weeks, many staff of all grades appear to be reliant on nothing but coffee, doughnuts, cake, energy drinks and sometimes cigarettes to keep them motivated. Some staff, particularly those of the longest service and more mature years (indeed the very ones who say work is no longer fun) appear to be lacking in fitness and may in fact be deemed unfit and in some cases, may we say, overweight.

It has therefore been decided that all junior and middle managers will be trained in choreography and after having been trained, they will organise daily team meetings where views can be expressed in interpretive dance.

This will have several benefits: staff will feel incentivised by the dedication of their managers; staff will feel free to express themselves in a new and enjoyable way; it will no longer be necessary to run annual stress-awareness or health-awareness weeks as this activity will not only eliminate stress but also increase fitness in the workforce.

Please note therefore that the company uniform will change very shortly to a unisex leotard to facilitate the interpretive dance. This will not in any way, diminish the importance of maintaining proper decorum in the office nor will it be in any way an excuse for lewd behaviour or remarks. Please note, the quality of your performance in interpretive dance will contribute to the level of any annual bonus.

In summary: Management has put in place measures for its staff to have fun and failure to have fun will result in disciplinary proceedings.

WHAT HAPPENED YESTERDAY

Supermarkets do not encourage introspection. In fact they are designed actively to discourage it. How could they make a profit if customers suddenly wondered what they were doing and whether they really did need all the meat and snacks and sugar which bombarded them after they'd sidled quickly and shamefully through the fruit and veg as if they represented a display of pornography.

Jane came in out of the rain and greeted the usually cheerful shop assistant at the temporary display. The shop assistant was staring out at the weather and came out of her reverie to smile wanly at Jane who was dripping onto the floor and trying to get her bags-for-life under some sort of control. It had been pouring for days and now a wicked wind was wrenching the last dead leaves off the trees so that they piled up in slimy rottenness underfoot. The supermarket was heaving and evidently everyone was in a vile mood.

Not for the first time, Jane wondered why her weekend seemed to consist almost entirely of buying food for her family, cooking for them, washing clothes for them, tidying up after them and trying to nag the children into doing some chores, some homework, help their father with the garden and finally endure the heartbreaking task of watching her teenage junk food obsessed daughter pick at the home cooked meal as if it was a plate of slugs.

The very affluence, extravagance and materialism of the supermarket was overwhelming. Last week, she had stood in the meat aisle, lobotomised by indecision, desperate to be anywhere else doing anything else, living alone eating toast and letting the family suffer for taking her for granted. Tears had sprung to her eyes and balancing on the narrow edge of her sanity, she stood lost with her trolley.

At least she felt like a whole person nowadays, able to go shopping without heaving one squirming toddler into a trolley seat while stopping the other toddler's sticky little fingers from touching everything, tempted by the sweet aisle and bright choking hazards dangling from pillars. You are both obtrusive and invisible when you go out with small children. You get in the way but you are mostly ignored, unless of course the children are playing up, when everyone and their dog glares at you as if you are the worst mother in history. Nowadays it was only teachers, complaining about the quality of her children's homework or lack of it, that implied parental inadequacy.

But here she was again, trying to work out what to cook which they'd all enjoy, how she could get some vegetables into her daughter, wondering if by any small miracle, the kids had either done their homework or their chores or both without being asked. Jane was aware there was more to life than this, but it perpetually eluded her. She wondered what her twenty-one year old self would have said if she'd realised all those plans to change the world had boiled down to wondering what to cook for dinner.

Finally she was in the toiletries aisle, trying to remember which shampoo was in favour this month and whether they were about to run out of toothpaste. A young woman stood motionless with her trolley impeding the flow of bad tempered damp shoppers. She was staring intently at something. It seemed to be the disposable nappies or maybe it was the formula or the baby bottles. Jane, unable to get round her for the moment, wondered what the issue was. As far as she could remember, you picked something when the baby was born and stuck with it, too exhausted or baffled to change. But the young woman was not making any kind of choice at all. Perhaps she was getting something for a friend or colleague. But suddenly she drew in her breath sharply and Jane heard the catch of a sob. She looked more closely at the stranger. Her eyelashes were wet with tears and she was turning to move away. Jane remembered. She remembered the day the blood came. Again. And again. Hope and then blood, hope and then blood. She recalled the sweet warm smell of her friends' children and the ice in her frozen, useless womb. She remembered the radio programme that made her have to stop the car, when they were talking about reading bedtime stories and she parked at the side of the road and cried, convinced she would never have children to read to.

Jane reached out to touch the younger woman but she was gone, swept off in the push of shoppers, pulling herself together, facing up to another wasted month. What could Jane have said anyway? 'It will be all right? It will work out?' maybe it wouldn't. In the end, it had worked out for Jane, but not for everyone. No, maybe it wouldn't be all right. Could she have said 'I understand?' Would that have helped? Jane was a lucky one.

Jane was in the way now. Sobered, she retraced her steps and bought both kids some rubbish to eat, then, remembering the shampoo her daughter wanted, she picked it up, trying not to wince at the price. She thought of her lovely son, head full of music and dreams and her lovely daughter, forthright but funny, both of them still willing to hug her, though her son now towered and her daughter could no longer fit on her hip. She had wanted to change the world, she had wanted to be important.

Well here she was, changing the world by loving her family, important to them, if to no-one else.

LETTER OF COMPLAINT

9th November

Dear Madam

COMPLAINT ABOUT DEFECTIVE IN-FORMATION

Thank you for your letter dated 5th November. I appreciate that you have made every effort to answer my complaint, however, I do not accept your conclusions and ask that you escalate this matter to the next level.

May I reiterate the issues:

I entered into this contract in good faith and understood that in order to get the model provided by you to operate at optimum efficiency, my responsibilities were as follows:

1. Ensure model is kept fed at all times, with top grade food
2. Ensure model is regularly lubricated with such fluids which suit best
3. Ensure model has an acceptably clean/tidy level of storage facilities/covering
4. Ensure model is not overworked
5. Ensure model's visual capacity units are not damaged by having to see an ugly operator and therefore having to maintain self (face and body)

6. Ensure model's audio capacity units are not over-loaded by excess nagging

In exchange I understood that the model would

1. Occasionally wash the dishes
2. Know how to operate a washing machine/work out the refuse collection schedule/be able to read a calendar to find out where I am without having to text me
3. Be generally useful round the house/garden
4. Maintain his own figure
5. Not snore
6. Keep my glass topped up if all else fails

May I set out again the worst aspects of the failure of this model to operate to the level expected when I entered into this contract:

1. Insists on chillies in absolutely everything even when it is a roast dinner
2. Falling asleep on the sofa half way through films and expecting me to explain them in detail when he wakes at the end credits
3. Leaving shoes, bags, boots, and on one occasion muddy jeans lying in public areas and complaining when they are moved/washed
4. Complete and utter failure to be useful around the house/garden
5. Keeps own glass topped up and says 'oh did you want some too?'

I do not accept the small print on the contract which brings to my attention that you cannot guarantee the model would meet the advertised outputs. I also do not accept the assertion that mowing the lawn five times a year and starting occasional DIY projects only to leave them half finished is equivalent to doing all the laundry, most of the cooking and cleaning and half the child rearing. Please find attached photographs showing the state of the garden and the bathroom in November 2015 (NB improvements started in April 2014 with a promise they'd be complete by Christmas. Admittedly, no guarantee was obtained as to which specific Christmas.)

I therefore concede that you are in breach of contract in that you did not prepare this model adequately for matrimony, or indeed adulthood and therefore request that you either take the model back for retraining or recompense me for the cost of colouring the grey hair and filling in the lines caused by stress.

Yours faithfully

Your Exhausted Daughter in Law

END OF THE LINE

The snow fell softly that day, dusting the train tracks, worrying the rail operators. But for the girl, it had been snowing inside steadily for a long long time and now her heart and her head were blocked with it and the lights had been dimmed by it. Not for her the pretty sparkle or the laughing amazing wonder of a snowflake; just the cold, the desperate endless cold, the knowledge it would never be warm again.

And so she took herself to the train track and made an end to the blizzard in her heart. And as the snow fell on reddened tracks, the driver and the police and the people who have to clear up, stood shivering, not just from the icy wind and the falling flakes but from the horror that was the end to a poor girl who preferred standing in front of a train to living one more day.

And at the stations the passengers waited. And waited. Not understanding the delay, watch checking, foot tapping, checking the news on their phones. And the news said and the news said… some celebrity is feeling down, someone's cat has been lost, the snow might cause disruption to timetables. But you had to hunt and hunt until you found the news that mentioned an anonymous girl who felt down, who felt lost, who couldn't make sense of anything except the train timetable anymore.

CANDY

'Well' said Hansel, 'this is a turn up for the books.'

Gretel kicked at the tree in frustration. 'Gor - and they promised us gingerbread, those kids.'

'Maybe it's red gingerbread,' Hansel suggested hopefully, 'or that strawberry stuff like liquorice strips only strawberry.'

His sister grunted sceptically, 'what was it they said we had to do?'

'We had to go in and be pathetic, they said. Then the old lady would let us eat the furniture or something.'

'Wot we gonna do that's pathetic?'

'Er… dunno. You're the one with the… what was the teacher said…. "uncontrollable imagination".'

Gretel sat down and thought about it for a bit. She chewed her lip and looked up into the branches for inspiration. A squirrel barked at her and dropped something on her head.

'OK I've got it, our parents - no, our dad and our evil step mum - took us out in the wood and left us there to *STARVE* to death,' she finished in lusciously sepulchral tones.

'Why would they do that then?' asked Hansel, thinking of his daft dad and cuddly stepmother.

'Cos there's not enough food for us and them and our baby brother. Our *half*-baby brother …her evil spawn.'

'What little Karlchen??'

Gretel sometimes found her brother exasperating. So he could mend things, but he couldn't imagine things. Still everyone had a cross to bear.

'Just pretend, Hansel. Just pretend. Look at it this way, according to those kids, she's a blind old ninny and we can pinch some, I don't know, barley sugar candlesticks or something and take them home to Karlchen to chew on.'

Hansel looked doubtful, 'isn't that lying?'

'No!' snapped Gretel, exasperated, 'it's pretending. It's different. Sort of. Sometimes. Anyway, do you want sweets or not?'

Sweets were in short supply at their house. Pretty much everything was, except work; which they had escaped today simply by running off when their stepmother was pre-occupied with the baby.

They inched their way up to the house. It was resolutely red. Not gingerbread. No candy canes round the door. No liquorice tiles. Hansel attempted a lick of the wall while Gretel knocked with the rapper. It was definitely not strawberry. He spat out resin and paint and a couple of ants.

The door opened with an ominous creak. Inside was darkness, except for a glow coming from the fire place and round the edges of the opening to a small iron oven.

Come to think of it, why hadn't those kids, if there was all those sweets to be had, why hadn't they eaten them all? Why had they told about it? They could have kept it secret and been munching on sofas and beds and tables for months. It was a big old house. Why had they been so keen to tell younger kids all about it?

'Come in little children,' said a croaky voice, 'you look tired and hungry - I might have something for you…'

Hansel looked at Gretel and Gretel looked at Hansel. Simultaneously they whispered 'LEG IT!' turned and ran for home.

'You're going to have to think up some excuse for why we didn't do our chores like we were supposed to,' gasped Hansel as they ran.

'I'm working on it,' panted Gretel.

The door screeched open a little wider. A young plump woman came out, watched the two children run away and shrugged. Then she coughed and put her hand to her throat. She'd be really glad when this laryngitis was gone and, closing the shrieking door, she'd be really really glad when Johannes oiled those flipping hinges.

But what she'd mostly be glad of was when she finally found out why all these small children kept turning up and knocking on her door and then running away.

PENALTY

'Look,' said the Tooth Fairy, 'All I want to know is have you asked the Elf and Safety Executive. Because I'm sure this is against regulations.'

'We've got to take our part in rehabilitation schemes, you know,' argued Will O' the Wisp, 'it's a cross doodah executive decision. Cross species, that's the thingummy.'

'Yes but why can't he stay with Santa? Look at him,' she gestured at the cowering burglar, 'He's about the right shape, he could act as stand in. Here - you - say ho ho ho.'

'Ho ho ho,' squeaked the burglar, his knees trembling.

'OK,' conceded the Tooth Fairy, 'so he needs training up.'

The reindeer put his head in his hooves and shook it.

'Yes but you're missing the point Toothy, Santa's just for Christmas. It takes more than twenty-four hours to rehabilitate an inveterate ne'er do well.'

'But why me?' she demanded, 'I mean - look at him, he's not exactly fairy-like is he? Can you imagine him in a tutu? And besides, I can't take him in all those kiddies' bedrooms, it wouldn't be right. I've had get a records check myself and carry a wing-cam to make sure it's all above board. And he's flabby. You need muscles to lift those sweet downy heads off their pillows - the little porkers. I blame junk food.'

Hobgoblin rubbed his hands together and smirked, 'You could let him look after the cash for you?'

'What cash? The little blighters' parents are total skinflints these days and as I get is some measly plaque covered tooth and 10% commission on whatever the parent is prepared to cough up. I remember when a shilling was a shilling and a sixpence got you twenty-four fruit salads, some crisps, a sherbet fountain and a comic. But not nowadays, oh no. 10p if I'm lucky. Sometimes it's a measly 2p. Can't even get wing glitter for that. I try to whisper in the kids' shell-like to try and get them to up the ante but no, they've all get head phones in. Anyway, I'm not giving a burglar my money bag. That's got to be off the scale in risk register terms.'

'Well someone's got to have him for the remaining seventy-six hours of his sentence,' Reindeer explained patiently, 'and Santa's gone to sleep now until 6th January and all except the Epiphany presents have been delivered.'

They sat in thought for a while, sipping their mead and watching the trembling burglar out of the corners of their eyes.

'I've got it!' yelled Will O' the Wisp making everyone jump, 'The Easter Bunny! He can help the Easter Bunny.'

'You've got to be joking,' argued the Tooth Fairy, 'It's only 25th December.'

'Exactly my thingy - point!' Will said triumphant, 'that means the supermarkets will need to get prepared for the next thing to fleece their customers for. He could paint some eggs.'

'Nah' said the Tooth Fairy, 'Too soon. Anyone got a better idea?' They all looked hard at the burglar, now weeping silently, wishing Santa had just left him to the mercy of the rottweilers in the house he had been burgling on Christmas Eve.

'You know,' said Reindeer thoughtfully, 'I reckon if you stripped him off, painted him gold, gave him some wings and a bow and some sort of posing pouch, he'd make a pretty good Cupid. Valentine's comes before Easter. I saw Valentine Cards up on Christmas Eve. He can give Cupid a hand. Get a few more people to fall in love, produce a few more kiddies, more money for my old mate Toothy'.

'I'll drink to that,' said the Tooth Fairy, raising her glass at the burglar, 'Bottoms up chum - community service ain't over yet.'

A SNOWY DAY

Snow came just before my eighteenth birthday. Snow so deep and widespread it blocked roads for miles. A souvenir paper was printed afterwards: photos of snow above door lintels, photos of the postman tramping for miles over snow, photos of dogs on hastily made sleds. Cars were abandoned on the motorway: drivers rescued by locals and put up in community centres. On foot, we trekked the three miles into town to buy bread and essentials - little groups trudging slowly. People called out cheerfully to strangers, helped each other up when they fell. In the little supermarket, the local radio was on - no music, just news. A helicopter had rescued a farmer's wife who'd gone into labour, neighbours rallied round their elderly neighbours, made sure they were safe. Snow's not going to get us down - we can recreate the Blitz spirit.

Our hill, you should have seen it. It was bad enough anyway, a double hairpin bend - drivers need to blast twice on the horn driving up or down. When it rained, you walked to school in a twisting torrent. When it snowed - no chance. If there had been a snow plough, it couldn't have got up. Anyway, our postman wasn't a hero. No way he was going to clamber up, then slip down for the sake of a hundred houses. So no birthday cards. No presents.

Lucky for me, it thawed just enough for us to get to the station so I could go for my university interview. The train was late and slow. The tracks had frozen and were now defrosting. We went up past flooded fields full of bloated sheep; drowned in the melt water. And then we changed direction.

But the snow hadn't melted in the North, so there we were, Mum and I, in totally the wrong clothes, looking out over a city which would have been strange even if it hadn't been sparkling white. The roads were clear but the pavements were slippery under my smart shoes and where the snow had been piled up into the gutter it was impossible to climb over in a narrow interview dress. A total stranger came up laughing, picked us up in turn and carried us to the other side of the road. Then we were on my own. The faculty house was up some uncleared side street. We crunched up to the door in sodden shoes, snow dusting our skirts. The secretary took Mum off for some tea while the Professor and I sat huddled over a gas heater to talk about English.

And so we returned from the still frozen North to the thawing South. The bloated sheep were hidden by the dark and our town was dripping with melted snow. And then here was home: warm and cosy, the lights in the dining room illuminating the diminished snowman in our front garden. The postman had been at last and finally, two weeks late, I had birthday presents to open.

THE LADDER

The angel went to Earth on a cold grey day and took up an assignment in a cold grey city full of cold grey unsmiling people.

For years he lived among them and tried to get them to see joy and light and love. He pointed out the flowers forcing their way through cracks in pavements and walls; unfurling leaves in dusty city parks; sunlight sparkling on the waves on the turgid river; the distant stars struggling against the orange night time glow and myriad office blocks. He pointed out the lovers and the families and the helping hands of strangers but for the most part people remained oblivious in their cold greyness: grumbling, dissatisfied, suspicious.

Year after year the angel plodded on leaving a glow and a flash of colour as he passed through discontented unwelcoming lives but slowly as his despair grew, he faded and his smile was replaced by tears. Heaven started to seem distant, a dream. His longing turned to agony until he could not bear to think of it. He felt each failure pinning his hidden wings to his side, each rejection seemed to be proof that he was no longer bright enough to return.

One day he stopped looking up. He sat on a bench and looked down at the ground and watched his feet slowly turning grey and cold. There was no point in going on. He might as well give up. Suddenly he realised that snow was falling, two flakes then three, the ground started to change to crisp clean white. He looked up and saw the whole city blanketed, the walls, the bridges, the paths. The people and cars and river all frozen in their tracks, glistening like diamonds, time stopped.

The angel stood up and looked round in amazement and saw not far away, a snow covered ladder disappearing into the sky and supported by nothing. The angel went over and tried to see to the top of the ladder but the sky was full of snow. Taking a deep breath, he started to climb, foot by foot. To start with he looked down past his grey feet on the icy rungs at the frozen city, full of people without joy, and and then he noticed that the air was warm and he could feel sun on his head and he raised his head. He had reached the top of the ladder and the sky was blue and hot and clean.

He looked at his hands and the grey was fading and he felt his wings flex under his coat.

'You are working so hard' a voice said gently, 'and you are exhausted. Bathe in love.'

The angel turned his face to the sun and smiled, he felt as if arms held him, as if he was resting his tired head on the steady beat of the heart of the universe. Then he looked down. Far below, at the foot of the ladder was the city, frozen in time, full of stubborn, patient, foolish, wise, nasty, lovely, cruel, kind, selfish, selfless people - all of them needing someone to shine like love in their grey world. The angel flexed his wings and then sighed. But he smiled too.

'Thank you,' he said, 'now, it's time to go back' and he descended the ladder, stepping off it as it disappeared and time started again for the people in the city, who laughed, amazed in the jewelled beauty of unexpected snow.

And the angel, recharged and full of warmth and love and colour took up his challenge once more.

ACKNOWLEDGMENTS AND GLOSSARY

With many thanks to Debbie Mathews and Emma McAllister, my reviewers, for their input and support.

Also many thanks to the wonderful members of 'Short Fiction Writers and Readers', 'Writers' Soapbox', 'Tales in Ten' and 'Flashnano - 30 stories in 30 days' Facebook groups for their inspiration and encouragement. In particular to Nav Logan who let me find an ending (or new beginning) for Avigail and David and Val Portelli who prompted 'I'm from the future and need your help'.

Welsh words: 'Croeso'- Welcome; 'Diolch' – Thank you.

OTHER BOOKS BY PAULA HARMON

About Paula Harmon
Paula Harmon, is a Chichester University graduate who has lived in Dorset since 2005. She is a civil servant, married with two children. Paula has several writing projects underway and wonders where the housework fairies are, because the house is a mess and she can't think why.

Please visit
www.paulaharmondownes.wordpress.com for short writing and book links.

Please visit **Paula Harmon's Amazon Author Page**

Murder Britannica
It's AD 190AD. Romano-Briton Lucretia is determined that her get-rich-quick scheme will not be undermined by minor things like her husband's death, dubious imposters or her married daughter's fascination with a celebrity gladiator. But when the deaths start to mount up, wise-woman Tryssa starts to ask questions.

The Cluttering Discombobulator
Can everything be fixed with duct tape? Dad thinks so. The story of one man's battle against common sense and the family caught up in the chaos around him.

The Advent Calendar
Christmas as it really is, not the way the hype says it is (and sometimes how it might be) - stories for midwinter.

The Case of the Black Tulips (with Liz Hedgecock)

When Katherine Demeray opens a letter addressed to her missing father, little does she imagine that she will find herself in partnership with socialite Connie Swift, racing against time to solve a mystery and right a wrong.

The Case of the Runaway Client (with Liz Hedgecock)

When Katherine and Connie take on a case at a music hall, they enter a new, exciting, and frightening world. Can they see through the glamour of the stage to find out what really happened to the missing star?

The Case of the Deceased Clerk (with Liz Hedgecock)

The Department recruit the duo to investigate London's mediums and mesmerists, several of whom are suspected of fraud. Katherine and Connie must pose as clients to discover what goes on behind closed doors.

Weird and Peculiar Tales (with Val Portelli)

Short stories from this world and beyond.

https://www.goodreads.com/Paula_Harmon
https://www.facebook.com/pg/paulaharmonwrites
https://twitter.com/PaulaHarmon789
viewauthor.at/PHAuthorpage

28472780R00082

Printed in Poland
by Amazon Fulfillment
Poland Sp. z o.o., Wrocław